The Stunted Man

The Stunted Man

By Ari Loeb

THE STUNTED MAN

Copyright ©2024 Ari Loeb
Abandoned House Books

Contact: www.ariloeb.com

Cover Design: Ari Loeb
Author Photo: Brittany Belz

ISBN: 978-1-7369939-5-8

First Edition, August 2024

9 8 7 6 5 4 3 2

For my brother, Adrian Jun Loeb.
Tortured heart. Lover of cats. Headbanger.

"I'm a creature of fine sensations."
—Mary Shelley, *Frankenstein*

NIGHTMARES

SNEAKY FUCKERS.

They only get sneakier.

I need a new drug every three weeks or so. This one's not doing it. Instead, I'm curled up in the back seat of this yellow cab, shivering and whining about the potholes and the disastrous fucking noise outside.

"Never take Amsterdam!" is what I mean to say, but what comes out is just a chalky gasp, because my throat feels like bitter white paste. Propranolol is supposed to be anti-anxiety. Yeah, this one's definitely not doing it.

Jake is in the front seat, talking to the driver. "Give me a pentagram, and I'll make you go faster," he says, to which I yell out, "No driver, don't give him a—" something, but I forget what I'm saying, and they can't hear me anyways over the metallic thunder that's exploding outside.

We need to get to Alfie's. Now. If they're still open. The potholes are bullying me, and I need to shit like it's the end of the world, probably because of the drugs, which I can't remember the names of anymore.

Amsterdam is purgatory.

"Hey, Jake," I say nonchalantly, as I cough five or six times. "Did you call Alfie's?"

He doesn't hear me. Jake is telling the cab driver about the benefits of drinking charcoal lemonade. "Hey," I repeat. "We're on Amsterdam, right? Where the hell are we?" Suddenly my head is clear, and I don't feel whiny anymore. "Is this fucking *Morningside?* Jake, isn't Alfie's on—whoa!" The cab stops. A pedestrian steps into the street near us.

Red light.

"Guys," I say calmly, hoping they can hear me over the earsplitting noise. "Can you turn up the air conditioning, please? I'm sweating my brains out back here."

They don't hear me. They really don't care. Jake is now explaining to the driver how if you smear mango oil all over your face, your pores will defend themselves against dirt and age.

"Guys," I persist. "Will you please turn up the AC?"

Nothing.

"My brain is leaking out of my nostrils, and this cab is like fucking donkey hell."

"What are you saying!" The driver shouts.

I answer back, completely cool. "I said . . . Columbus runs *downtown*. I thought I heard Jake tell you to take Columbus. Sorry, that's my bad."

The driver accepts this, although he's eyeing me with a shocked, terrified expression in the rearview mirror.

"Hey, Lex!" Jake says to me, turning around, and I immediately don't want his attention anymore, or the driver's, who's still staring at me. "When did you get here?" Jake always takes the front seat. Such a Midwesterner.

A woman walks past my window, and I jerk, almost smacking my head into the roof of the cab. "What?" I say. "It's a car. I was here when we got in. And, oh yeah, did you call Alfie's? *That* was what I meant to say."

"Yes, Lex, I called Alfie's," he says. "We're all good."

"Oh, good," I sigh. "I feel a lot better."

I'll probably have nightmares tonight. Something about suspicious, evil cab drivers and disastrous noise. I pull a pint of Early Times whiskey out of my jacket and take a gulp.

"You can't drink alcohol in here, sir!" the driver yells.

I manage to say, "Well, you can't talk on your phone in here, but I ain't complaining."

"I wasn't on the phone!" He says, but I can't hear him through all the cacophony. For the moment my throat feels better. I know we're close to Alfie's now, and I'm glad I'll never see this cab driver again.

Somehow, it's even louder in the restaurant than outside. Maxwell is behind the bar, and I throw him a negligent wave, never breaking my march to the bathroom, where my ass proceeds to party like it's 1999. When I return to the dining room, Jake is sitting with Aurora in a booth by the window. The restaurant is not very crowded, despite all the porcelain clanging and fervid conversations that tremble like a Broadway theater on opening night. Underneath it all, Katy Perry trying to be music.

"I love this place," I say as I sit down next to Jake. "What's up, Aurora?"

"You guys are late," she says. "This is my third drink."

"Had to lend some equipment to a friend."

Aurora looks puzzled. "You lent your safety equipment to someone?"

"Yeah, it's OK," I say. "Anyways, I'm not using it. And it's hard to find a harness in my size."

"You lent someone your harness? That's your lifeline! What if it gets damaged?"

"It's fine," I explain. "If I can't damage my lifeline, no one can."

Aurora stops twirling the ice in her glass and looks at me. "I'm worried about you, Lex."

"He's just having a bad day," Jake says. Then to me, "What, I'm allowed to say that. You were complaining the whole way here. You need to double your dosage. Or like, meditate more."

"What I need is a job," I say.

Jake rolls his eyes. "We're still hiring at Harlem Public," he says. "Why don't you work there?"

"I'm not a waiter, Jake."

"Bartenders, man! It's good money. Girls everywhere. Alcoholics have respect—you'll fit right in!"

I hold my index fingers next to my head while sneering, making a ram-of-the-devil face at Jake.

He's right.

"Come on, Lex, it's a job," Jake says. "The universe is manifesting. What are you so afraid of?"

"Earthquakes," I say. "And my show closing."

"Be serious."

Aurora looks at Jake. "He is being serious."

"I'm not doing it," I say. "That's an unhealthy work environment for me." I touch my beard and twiddle it a little bit. "Now I'll ask again. What's up, Aurora?"

Aurora and I have been friends for years. Long years on the road, and as roommates. I'd call her my wingman, my sanity. She's actually a better friend than Jake.

Jake is mostly gay, but he's been together with Aurora since their college days at Pace before I met them. We all used to tour together with various dance companies. Mark Morris, mostly. We lived together on 139th Street, just next door to where I live now. Those were eight good years. We were successful dancers in New York, something we had always dreamt about. But the money was incongruent with the cost of living. Even in the best of times, we were four of us in an apartment, with one bathroom. In the worst of times, there was no food to eat and paradoxically, too many rats and roaches.

Eventually I got Wolfblood the cat, and she helped eat the roaches. I should have named her Renfield. Wolfblood, my sweet love kitten. She ate the roaches while the roaches ate—I don't fucking know.

"Hey, let's go to Reunion," I say, putting my fork down and wiping the elk sauce off my beard with a napkin. At Reunion the drinks are cheap, and as of now, my bottle is dry.

"Now?" Jake says.

"Yeah, I have a feeling."

Aurora looks at me suspiciously and says, "Yeah, I have a feeling too."

Jake thinks about it for a moment, then points his fork at me, lobster bit dangling off the end like a dripping question mark and says, "No, I can't go."

"Why not?" I say.

"I need to finish these tarot cards I'm working on," he says. "I have seventy-eight designs, all different. I told you about this. But what's this feeling you guys are having?"

"I don't know," I say.

"Yeah, if we knew what it was, we wouldn't call it a feeling," Aurora adds.

"I have a feeling I left my bike there last night."

"Oh," Jake says. He eats the lobster bit. "You guys go ahead. I have to get as much work done as I can before Mercury goes into retrograde."

So, we agree to part ways.

After paying the check, Aurora and I walk the two blocks to Reunion.

"I don't dance!" I'm shouting at the girl—a blunt, disappointing punchline.

She's smiling wryly at me, snaking back and forth to the retro-style music that's pulverizing us from all angles. But her young eyes don't understand. Her smile slips a cog, like a shoddy clutch.

"I have a thing!" I add.

Her smile comes back, although now she's in first gear again. To her it's a lame joke. The chicken crossed the road because it didn't want to dance with her. Reunion is packed, dark and cloistered in a haze of sweat and booze. The music sways, crushes.

Aurora speaks up, "Don't say that, you weirdo!" Then, to the stranger, "He's like, a professional dancer."

The girl boosts into second. "Really?"

"Yeah, well, I was." I'm touching my beard to make sure there isn't anything stuck in it. "Now when I get the urge to dance, it just kinda goes away as soon as I start moving."

"Bullshit!" says Aurora.

"I'm pretty sure you can dance!" says the stranger. "I wanna see!"

I'm looking at her body that smells like candy and vodka, tiny and squiggly in a too-tight black dress and I'm thinking *I wish I could fucking dance.* This stranger looks like no one I've ever slept with before, cheekbones on the moon, almost Native American.

Aurora likes her too. Aurora likes just about everyone that I like.

"Sorry, I'm not dancing," I say. "I'm more of a metal guy." And why not? Metal is so passe it's practically in again.

She's not a great dancer, but she's convincing as hell, pinned in fourth gear, now purring like a lioness. Finally, I surprise myself with an unexpected witticism. "I have two left dicks!" I scream.

"What?" She can't hear me over the noise.

"I have two . . . It's like I have two left feet, but . . . I'm gonna go get a drink! Do you want a drink?"

Aurora keeps the stranger engaged while I go to the bar. I've bought myself five or ten minutes.

The bar is crowded, but I'm able to get a drink without waiting. People always move out of my way. They don't know they're doing it. I'm told I vibrate. I order an IPA for myself, a tequila ginger for Aurora, and a vodka tonic for the stranger. Yes, I can smell what she's drinking. I'm that good.

I remind myself that unemployment should start back up in a couple of weeks, so I'll be OK.

The stranger is still dancing with Aurora. "Hey!" she yells at me, and I can see she's starting to sweat. "Aurora tells me you were an acrobat, too!"

"Long time ago." I'm always blushing.

"Come on, you're not that old," she says.

I blink.

"Show me some moves!"

10

When people shout at me to "show them some moves," the first thing that comes to mind is shoving a broadsword up their ass and screaming, "Valhalla!" But for some reason this girl doesn't do that to me. She thinks I'm special, so I'm feeling pretty good about her. I can move in a little now that there's something solid to hang everything else on.

"I don't dance anymore," I say, coyly this time.

"I don't believe you," she says, grinning.

Aurora gives me a wink.

"Nah, look at me, I'm a bear."

"A *dancing* bear!"

"Look, I have a better idea." I glance at Aurora. "Let's take a cruise on my bike. Aurora can sit on the back, and you can sit on the gas tank. You're small enough."

The stranger thinks about it. To rescue her from the horror of making a decision, I cut back in with, "Hey, what's your name?"

"Halona!" she says. She pushes her hair back out of her face, and I can smell her shampoo. Gardenias, a white flower in pure black hair.

"That's sweet," I say. "What's it mean?"

"Nothing to you!" Aurora shouts, dancing.

Halona glances at Aurora. "It's Iroquois," she says. "It means happy fortune."

I wipe my sweaty hands on my jeans. "Of course it does," I say. "Come take a ride with us. Riding is more fun than dancing."

Halona considers this. "What do you do with your bike in the winter?" she asks.

"I keep it in my apartment."

Her eyebrows go up, as if visualizing the size of my apartment. "Doesn't it smell bad?"

"I love the smell," I say. "I can smell motorcycles all day long."

"And I bet you do!"

I can't think of where I'm going from here, but Halona's already moving with me toward the doors. Aurora slams her tequila and trails after us.

It's late, and there isn't any traffic.

Sepultura screams from my Harley's speakers, as we merge onto the West Side Highway, then switch to Riverside Drive near the Boat Basin at 79th St., soaring north in the direction of my apartment. Halona's hair is practically blinding me, blinding my mind. I want to hug her, but Riverside Drive is a truck route, and I've had a few drinks, and my sweaty hands are on the handlebars.

We come to a stone, columnal war monument, which stands triumphantly on 89th Street by the river. It's one of the only places in Manhattan with empty space, even at 2 a.m. We sit on the steps, and I pull out a joint.

"You've really transformed," Halona says. "You were a dancer in Cirque du Soleil?"

"Not hip-hop," I say, because I hate being cliche. "I was on Broadway, too."

"No shit."

"Yeah, that was a weird time. Lotta cocaine."

"What happened? Like, what caused the transformation?"

"Well, I've been dancing since I was a kid, you know? I trained in ballet."

"You?" She shoulders me playfully. "No way."

"Yeah, and I toured for about ten years. Then I settled in New York and got a job on Broadway. Choreographing and performing."

"What show?"

"Spider-Man."

"You're Spider-Man?"

"You have a lot of energy." I poke her stomach gently. "What did you take?"

"Nothing! Hold on. *You're—*"

"I'm part of the multiverse, yeah. I was skinnier back then."

"Wait." She's doing the math. "How old are you?"

Our eyes disengage. "Oh, we'll get to that, darling."

I gaze at the Hudson River in what I hope looks like reverie. Aurora is crouched by the river wall, inspecting something on the bottom of her shoe. "Anyways, the world changed," I say. "The arts changed. New York changed. And of course, I changed. I got tired of being on the same track all the time. So, I threw away my tights and got a bunch of tattoos instead. I started to feel more like myself." The moon is low, large, and yellow over Jersey. "This is my first real beard."

Halona is closing her eyes, engrossed by the warm nostalgia rolling off the river, the high of the bike ride, the nearness of my voice. "But what really changed?" she says softly. "Like, what happened?" Her dark eyes slowly open.

"It's actually really silly."

"What is?"

"Well . . . OK," I take a deep breath. "I was watching *Breaking Bad* one night, and I was super high and bleary, like one eye closed, but the other one transfixed. Walter White was saying to Jesse, 'Hit the reset button, Jesse. You're *young*. I can't do it, but you can. Hit the reset button!' And I was in delirious rapture, thinking, 'Yeah, hit the reset button, dude.' The next morning, I punched a hole in the fucking reset button. I was tired of New York, tired of the arts, and I wanted to start over."

"Wow."

"Yeah. When I woke up the next day, everything seemed old and ramshackle. I was reborn somehow. Ingeminated."

"Did you learn all these big words in dance class?"

Since I'm right in the middle of inhaling the joint, I'm forced to spray smoke out of every orifice and then cough for two whole minutes. Finally composed, I decide to do the short version: "Anyways, I packed up my stuff, picked up my cat and jumped off the fire escape. I moved back home to Los Angeles and started over as a stuntman."

"A *stuntman!*"

"Despite my fear of earthquakes."

While Halona and I continue talking, Aurora stands at the riverbank, staring at Jersey City, smelling the river, and feeling the shockwaves. She's heard all this before.

Thousands of windows line the Hudson, far removed but always there, like ideas in the back of your mind. The mind is a hotel with infinite rooms, its guests folded in throughout time, most of them concealed from our daily consciousness. The doors are all closed, but sometimes they open.

I don't want to sleep with Halona anymore, even though it would be so easy because she's so small. I *do* want to sleep with her, but not now. Not tonight.

"I'm gonna want to take you home soon," I slur.

"Just like that?" she retorts.

"No, not just like that. I'm tired. Look, Halona, I do a lot of drugs. And now it's that time of night when I'm locked out of everything. I'm in the dead zone, and I'm not coming out."

"That's a weirdly beautiful thing to say," she says. Then, ignoring my suggestion that we leave, she asks, "What's your earliest childhood memory?"

At first, I don't respond. I can't seem to remember anything from early childhood. Not a cartoon, a pet, or even a mailman. Then it hits me. Knocks me over, more like.

"Nightmares," I say.

I'm more perplexed by this than surprised. "I must've been four years old. *Sesame Street* was flooded. The characters were all running around, and a red Muppet named Telly was newscasting. He looked distressed, hair splayed like pipe cleaners. Telly was staring at me, reading the news, and his eyes were wide, flat, and panicked. A killer whale was loose in the streets. News footage showed the whale as it swam through the flood. It twisted, raising each black pectoral fin out of the water, then slapped the surface with deafening bangs. These bangs got closer and louder, until they became gunshots, and the gunshots were everywhere.

"I can't believe I'm remembering this," I say. "I've always sort of remembered, but I've never taken the time to hash it out." I look away from the river, from the myriad windows of Jersey City and the low-lying gold moon, back to Halona.

She's giggling to herself. "*Sesame Street* gave you nightmares?"

"Everything gives children nightmares!"

"I know, but look at you. Big, tattooed man. *Stunt*man. And *Sesame Street* gave you nightmares?" She leans back, reclining on the monument steps, and looks up at me, her dark eyes glimmering.

"That's not all," I say. "Remember the Count? The purple Dracula Muppet? He was *counting all the gunshots!*" I say it like it's funny, but I don't think it's funny.

Halona's giggles boil into full laughter. "You should go back and start your childhood over," she says.

"I'm a stuntman," I say. "That's pretty much the same thing."

Halona finishes the joint and offers me the roach. I shake my head no, so she stubs it out on the steps.

"You know what the really spooky part about that nightmare is?" I say, leaning closer over her face. "When I watch the news, and I see the reporters with that manufactured glower on their faces, like Jake Tapper or whoever, I remember Telly the red Muppet, staring flatly at me, frozen in shock. *Sesame Street* gave me nightmares, and nightmares gave me CNN."

Halona rolls her eyes, turns her head, and notices Aurora. She's trying to scale the monument, bracing herself between two pillars. "Is that your girlfriend?" she says.

I don't like that Halona called Aurora "that" instead of "she," but I understand women well enough to not be put off.

"No," I say. "Aurora is Jake's girlfriend." She doesn't believe me, so I elaborate. "Jake's a very old friend. He and Aurora have been welded together since childhood. During the war in Iraq, all the scrap metal in New England was melted down to make weapons for the war effort. Aurora and Jake were accidentally melted down with all the metal, and they've been inseparable ever since."

That was a stretch. But that's how I talk at this hour.

Halona blinks at me slowly. "You're metal," she says.

And just like that, I like her again.

"Hey, let's get ready to go," I say. Halona looks at me but doesn't move. "Come on, stand up. Shake it out." I look towards Aurora, who has come down from the pillars to gaze at Jersey City again. She's quietly swaying to music that's in her head, her left hand clutching a green beer bottle. I have no idea where she got that beer from. I look back down at Halona and say, "Anyways, my cat has allergies. We gotta go."

"Oh!" she says, surprised, and then either for lack of words, or some other reason, she hugs me. Unsure of what to do with myself I stand up and yell, "Hey *sexpot!*" over to

Aurora. She takes a sip from her beer while turning around. "Want a ride?"

Aurora says she'd rather walk. That's no shock. She and Jake live on 85th Street, only five blocks away. This war monument is where we meet when I pick her up to do stuff.

Halona says, "You're pretty cool," which causes me to blush. It's thirty seconds before I realize she said it to Aurora and not me.

On the ride to her apartment in the East Village, Halona's rubbing my chest and torso under my shirt, with hands like wild hyenas scampering over the blustery plains of Africa. She touches my crotch, and I'm spontaneously changing my mind about not fucking her. I reach back with my throttle hand and stroke her leg.

Then the darkness comes.

I can remotely place pulling up to Halona's building. It was old and shitty, like Nineties Essex St. dilapidated shitty. I don't think it's strange at all, forgetting momentarily that Essex St. is now high-rises, fluorescent-lit pharmacies, and yoga studios. Cupcake shops and shit. That doesn't cross my mind. But somehow what I'm seeing is a mix of dirty Delancey Street intersecting Essex Stay-the-fuck-away Street, superimposed on some sci-fi utopia.

And I remember my bike chain. Twenty-pounder. I was holding it, tying up my tires. I remember holding Halona's hair, almost clutching it, black gardenias, my erection dancing through four dimensions. My ass and legs were about to surge like some cosmic volcano . . .

I don't remember anything else.

I don't remember riding home.

THE STUNTED MAN

HOME

CRASHING THROUGH THE front door of my apartment, I immediately get the bottle of Dewar's from the kitchen. Blue Label, this time.

It's no use going to bed without first rinsing the alertness off my brain. That, and the metallic taste of Riverside Drive, which is pleasant while you're there, but leaves a sediment in your mouth. A biker's ritual, perhaps.

My cocaine is in the bedroom, so I toss my jacket and boots on the couch and head that way. But I stop halfway to the bedroom and turn back toward the kitchen, deciding a glass would help the whiskey go down. If I'm lucky, I'll drink less than half the bottle tonight. I fill a small glass with amber scotch, drink half of it, then pretend I have a gentleman-size drink and take that over to the bedroom where I cut up a small vampire fang of coke on an old Kanye CD case—the one with the demonic teddy bear on the back. The case is ruddy and blurry from years of cocaine usage, although I've never actually heard the album. I don't know where the case came from.

So, I slip into the secret night, where the pretty colors of the day fall away, and the face underneath has no nose and a bottomless, black mouth and bulging eyes. It's the face you don't see because it's only there when you're asleep. Most people have dreams, either good ones or bad ones, then wake up in the morning feeling more or less OK. Others, like me, choose to look the gorgon in the eye, and endure that cold stoniness all night long.

When I wake up, threads of pain are everywhere, veining my face and body. Red, like evil rivers running backwards.

Someone is moaning beside me, some kind of monster breathing. I realize it's my phone vibrating. When I manage to find it, a surge of hope rolls through me, as an important yet unexpected name floats above the screen.

Ed Fury?

I mutter, "Fuck," but it spirals into a coughing fit, so I put the phone down and wait out the vibrations in shame. I'll have to call him back as soon as I can speak. Ed Fury isn't a guy you want to keep waiting around. Soon, my initial hope drops into panic. There isn't a stunt coordinator more intimidating than Ed Fury.

It's 8 a.m., which means it's work-related. He probably wants to give me a job.

I usually micro-dose a muscle relaxer when I sleep because I grind my teeth at night. But last night I didn't, and my teeth feel awful.

I roll out of bed like a slowly capsizing canoe.

Suddenly, I remember Halona—how small and agreeable she was—and a powerful lust floods with regret, which doesn't mix well with my hangover and causes me to put both my hands on the wall and stare at the floor. A familiar swelling in my esophagus, followed by hot and cold prickles all over my skin.

I shamble into the bathroom and check the mirror. My face looks like a raw turkey, eyes the color of roadkill and fluttering slightly. *Not bad*, I think. But when I see all the blood in my piss, a counterargument drifts in. And as I flush the pink-stained water down, I straighten my back, wincing at the tight, disciplinary warning in the middle of it. I moan, trying to wake up my vocal cords, but as I open my mouth vomit shoots out and I collapse over the toilet. Liquid splashes up into my face and eyes, but I don't care about that because my back has gone out. Stony fingers clutch me from behind. Nerves split apart, and I fall the rest of the way down, landing on my cat, who screams and scurries away, leaving me alone in a scrambled heap on the floor.

After ten minutes I start to mewl, then slowly bring myself to a sitting position. It's hot in my apartment, but I'm freezing, forcing myself not to shiver because my back feels like it's being crushed. I take shallow breaths, trying not to move. At least my voice is warm from mewling. There's a small victory in that.

Another ten minutes go by, and I'm fully committed to spending half the day on the floor, which is fine. But I have to call Ed Fury back before I can completely submit.

So, I crawl.

I crawl like hell to the kitchen, where I draw five shots of espresso that I drink with six Advil and two Tylenol, and a glass of cold milk. I also feed my cat, Wolfblood. Then I walk slowly back to the bedroom to call Ed Fury.

He answers right away and screams, "What's up, bro!"

"What's up, bro!" I yell softly. "How's it been, dude?" I'm moving back to the bathroom, waddling like a man made of rusty shovels and vomit.

"It's great, dude! You know, just doing my thing."

"Cool."

"Yeah, listen. I'm prepping a show right now. What's your availability like for the next three months?"

"Um . . ." I pretend to think about it. "Pretty good!" I quickly stick my phone in a towel and vomit into the sink. My back screams in sacrifice, but Fury doesn't hear it.

"Yeah?" he says.

"Yeah, I mean I have a few mocap gigs next week, but nothing that's officially booked," I lie.

"Sweet, bro! So, I'm working on this film. It's the new *Frankenstein*. Ben Schilling is playing Frankenstein's monster."

"That's great," I say. "I just read *Frankenstein* three weeks ago." This time I'm not lying. I actually did read *Frankenstein,* although it was more like six months ago.

"Oh yeah?" he says. "That's perfect. So, Ben Schilling is really into the idea of having a movement specialist. To help him with the embodiment of his character. It starts in two weeks and goes until late September."

I have no idea what day it is. Late May sometime. I say, "Sweet."

"Yeah, so, you think you're available?"

"Definitely, bro. What do you need from me?" I puke again, but not much comes out. The room is swaying, and the floor is three miles away.

"Well," he says, "I'm meeting with the producers in an hour. I'll let them know you're available, and I'll call you back. How does that sound?"

A chunk of vomit is lodged in my sinuses, but I'm too weak to get water.

"It sounds dope," I say. "Where does it work?"

"We're shooting in New Orleans."

"That's awesome," I say, and then quickly add, "I'm a New York hire."

"Of course, bro! Don't worry about that. I got you."

Hearing Ed Fury say, "I got you" is like hearing a speeding train say, "Stay there on the tracks, and I'll go around you!" I don't exactly believe him. He's kind of a crackhead. Ed Fury's stunt business is called "Barbaric Fury," and to his credit, I think that's a good name. A little high-and-mighty, but a good name for what it is. At least he knows that I'm a

New York hire, and not a local. This means first-class air tickets, a nice hotel, per diem, and maybe a rental car. Good shit. I'm probably gonna get paid for puking today.

"This is dope," I say. "Thanks so much for the call."

"Of course, bro!" he says again. "Meantime, can you send me your movement coaching reel? And whatever else you got?"

"Yes, sir," I say. But I don't actually have a coaching reel. I absolutely suck at promoting myself. "But you'll have to give me until this afternoon. I'm at the gym right now, and I have to look for that stuff on my hard drive."

Fury assures me that that's fine. And when he mentions something about my allergies, I realize I haven't breathed through my nose all morning. I say something in agreement, something about it being late May. My vision blurs while an apprehensive silence fills Fury's end of the line, so I add, "Thanks so much for thinking of me," and I do feel thankful, even though I can't figure out why he called me in the first place, as my back is fused to the bathroom wall, sliding at a snail's pace toward the floor.

"Of course, bro!" Fury says. "I gotta go. Send me that stuff. Let's fucking do this!"

"Yes, sir," I exclaim. "Talk soon, bro."

Now I'm sliding all over the bathroom wall, sweat running off my torso and legs in streams. It's another ten minutes before I can stand up, grasping the basin as a crutch. I look disgustedly into the sink where eight undigested pills have wedged themselves into the drain, clogging it. I wonder vaguely: if I vomit up pure stomach acid, will it digest the pills and unclog the sink? Instead, I run some water on it and leave the bathroom. My only objective is to get myself near the air conditioner in the bedroom.

I waddle like a wooden penguin back to the bedroom. My boxer shorts are soaked with sweat, my nostrils caked with scabs, which means cocaine is not an option, unless I smoke it.

Kneeling at the side of my bed in a prayer position, my thoughts are directionless, a mental rainstorm. I've wasted the coffee and pills, and it's too difficult to try that again. I'm going to be kneeling here all day.

I wonder if I'm capable of putting a demo reel together for Fury. Yes, I certainly am, but it's going to be a crappy one. The thought of joining Barbaric Fury is about as alluring as riding my motorcycle off a cliff and plummeting into a sea of cat shit.

Who's going to watch Wolfblood while I'm in New Orleans?

I shouldn't be thinking about that now. First, I need to figure out this demo reel dilemma, and how to put copious amounts of Advil back into my system.

I remember that I have some zombie movement footage from *The Walking Dead,* back when I lived in Atlanta, and all kinds of test footage from the animated sections of *Ready Player One.* If I mix that up with some *Terminator* footage, I can whip together a 60-second creature movement reel. Add in my resume and stunt reel, which I haven't updated in five years, and it should be a good enough package for Fury.

I can't even think about Adobe Premiere, so I open iMovie on my laptop, still kneeling at the side of my bed, and an hour later I've sent everything to the boss.

Five minutes go by. Then my phone buzzes, a (310) number displayed on top. My vision has improved from triple to double—a sign of hope. But my hollow, roiling stomach still reels at strange moments, trying to flush my soul down some swirly cosmic toilet.

"Hello?" I say, studiously.

"Hi, Alex? This is Patricia, I'm a producer on *Everyone's Frankenstein*. Ed Fury gave me your number."

"Hi Patricia, nice to meet you."

"Yes, same to you," she says. "I'd like to check your availability through September nineteenth. Do you have any conflicts or anything?"

"No, ma'am," I say. "After this week I'm totally free."

"Great! So, the director David Morley and I are going to Vegas tomorrow to meet with Mr. Schilling. Then Wednesday we have a Zoom meeting with Morley, Ed Fury, and Mr. Schilling. Can we count on you to join the Zoom meeting?"

"Of course!"

"Great," she says. "The time isn't confirmed yet. It depends on Mr. Schilling's availability, so hopefully you can accommodate that?"

The fan in my air conditioner is rattling like a shoddy muffler. I think about suicide for a moment, then decide I should focus on the movie instead. I can't do math, but my subconscious whispers the number *eighty thousand dollars* in my mind.

"Absolutely fine," I say. "I'll blackout the whole day. I mean, I'll *block* out the whole day. Just let me know when a time is set."

"Perfect," she says. "In the meantime, can you email me your movement specialist rate, along with your contract info?"

"Absolutely," I say, and then quickly add, "I'm a New York hire."

She laughs. "That's fine. Just send me your rate and contract info. I'm texting you my email address now."

"Perfect," I say. "Sounds good."

"This is exciting!" she says. "Ben fucking Schilling!"

I don't care much for celebrities, so I say, "I know! I seriously hope this works out!"

We end the conversation, and now I have a new problem. I don't know what my rate is. "Movement specialist" isn't even a real job, at least not according to SAG. So, I call my friend, Arrow. He's another stunt coordinator, but he's not as frightening or aggressive as Ed Fury.

How did Fury get the idea to call me in the first place? I thought he hated me. I've worked with him twice before, and he was very obvious about how he'd felt. Fury's stunt team is highly competitive, all of them topsiders, the most badass and in-demand stunt players—which I know I am not. He's the last guy I'd expect to avail me.

Arrow answers the phone, and I explain the situation.

"Fury?" he says. "Be careful, dude."

"I know. I've worked with him before. Fucking blow-hard."

"Totally," Arrow says. "That guy loves to talk about himself."

"Yeah. And he hates when other people talk about *themselves.*"

"Oh good, so you're already prepared. Hey, isn't Fury the guy who ripped out Rachel's hair on *Black Lagoon?*"

"Yup."

Arrow thinks about it for a moment, then says, "Just give them the highest number you can think of."

"But what if they say no?" I say. "The way the producer was talking, it sounds like it's super low budget. One of Ben Schilling's more, um, practical films."

"Hold on, I'm looking it up right now." Keyboard clatter on Arrow's end of the line. "A hundred and forty million, according to IMDb."

"That's pretty good," I say.

"Dude, you know Fury's making like four hundred grand on this movie. Worst they can say is no."

"But that's what I'm saying. What if that's the end of the conversation?"

"Well, you need to know your worth, dude. You're Lex fucking Mercier, and you're amazing. They need you on this. Fuck them. Give them a high rate."

My phone buzzes in my hand. Patricia.

"Yeah, OK," I say. "Look, I just got the script. I'm gonna read it really quick. Maybe it'll give me an idea of what kind of um, work . . . I'll be doing."

"Perfect!" he yells. "Good job, man. You deserve this."

We hang up.

The script takes forever to read, but it's very good. It's funny, and super violent. The whole visual theme is blood. Death metal, from hair to boots. There's even an undead villain called the "Dead Assassin." I'm so fucking in.

I send Patricia an email with my movement specialist rate and contract info.

Five minutes later, Ed Fury calls me back. He explains that my movement specialist rate is barely higher than a stunt contract, and I should be asking for more. I reply with something vague, tossing numbers into the air. I tell him that after reading the script, it looks like they're only going to bring me on for a week, maybe two, so it doesn't really matter what I'm making. Fury hesitates, perhaps intentionally. Then he offers to put me on a stunt contract and carry me through the whole run of the film, which causes me to stand up from the side of my bed, despite the pain, which feels like I'm being crushed sideways somehow.

"That's fucking awesome!" I say. "I wasn't going to ask for that. Fuck, yes!"

"Hell yeah," he says. "Glad to have you on board, buddy."

"Let's fucking go!" I scream.

"Let's fucking go!" he screams back.

"Can I still ask for more money?"

"No, dude. You fucked that one."

We end the call, and I gimp-walk back to the kitchen. Without thinking, I pour myself what's left of the Dewar's bottle, take a delicious gulp, then turn to walk back to the bedroom where I can lie down. But the floor wobbles and I shudder, dropping the glass. It shatters at my feet, as my knees disengage, and I collapse onto the living room floor. An edge of glass finds its way into my side, and I already know I'm bleeding. But I can't move, and I'm in too much pain to pass out. Suddenly my nose is clear, capillaries reaching towards the smell of blood and scotch.

The wail of sirens on 139th Street goes on forever. Endless ambulances, destined for everywhere, coming for everyone, eventually.

But not here.

Not now.

As I descend into a semiconscious doze, half-crying because I want breakfast and I know I'm never going to get it, it occurs to me that I might be in over my head.

I'm already regretting what I'm about to do.

WOLFBLOOD

MY BACK IS locked, tight.

The floor of my apartment is cold, so I focus on that.

Eventually, lying sprawled on my back, thoughts begin to form.

Halona.

Gardenia-scented black hair.

Some kind of movie.

Holy shit, I'm bleeding.

Wolfblood is standing in front of me, tail twitching with relief. Such an odd emotion to show while your man is, well . . . like this. I reach out, although it pains me, and knuckle her face a little. She immediately starts purring. My hands are the color of old pumpkins, and at first, I don't know why.

Then I remember the night before. The scotch, the cocaine, and the Advil. Phone calls with producers, and . . . Ed Fury?

I roll onto my side, half stuck to the floor with blood, thinking I have some healing to do if this is going to work at all. Rain clouds have darkened the sky, rendering my apartment a sullen, quiet blue. It must be after noon by now.

I begin to weigh my options, doing my best to think. But my mind is full of snakes and holes, and Wolfblood is an extremely loud purrer, so all I can come up with is an abbreviated list of pros and cons.

There are two pros that stand out to me. Money, and the opportunity to feel relevant again, which somehow seems more important than a paycheck. I haven't worked in five months, ever since *The Lesser Dead* series wrapped. Since then, I've been drinking from plastic jugs. The bottle of Dewar's was a splurge—a reaction to an unexpected residual check. If I book this job, I can earn enough cash to move out of New York City for good. Maybe retire from stunts and do something better for the world.

The cons list is a bit longer. I have twelve herniated discs in my spine—something only a doctor in Connecticut and I know about. And because my hips are rusted through, it takes five or six seconds for me to stand up. I'm an aging stuntman, well past my prime. I don't even train anymore. All the years of circus arts and dance and stunts have ground me down. I've left sweat and skin cells on over five hundred stages, dashed my body against two hundred television shows, and the remaining wreckage that is Lex Mercier has been brining in alcohol for years. Three months on a full-scale action movie will be difficult, perhaps impossible. Also, Wolfblood's allergies are worsening daily, and she has conjunctivitis, and feline herpes, which are exacerbated by stress. If I leave her in New York, she might just unravel and die.

Then there's the less obvious hang-up: I have a mild drug problem. It's manageable, but it stems from anxiety. I have been known to disappear for days at a time. One time, after being AWOL for eight days I awakened to discover I'd been fired from a job I hadn't known I'd had. Over a hundred text messages were on my phone. Remembering this makes me laugh. Part of me is amused by the thought of a film crew looking for me while I float down the Mississippi into the Gulf of Mexico, alligators getting stoned off my drug-laced corpse flesh. The larger part of me, however, is not amused, and a trembling paranoia starts creeping in.

I slide my hands along the linoleum floor, feeling for my phone in a lazy imitation of a snow angel. My hand grazes Wolfblood, and she stands up, walks around to face me. Her eyelids are a dark purplish color, her forelegs ragged from over-grooming, a reaction to her allergies and stress. I finger the pale patches of skin on her ankles. She steps away self-consciously.

Eventually I find my phone, which is full of bad news.

Firstly, there are no rain clouds darkening the sky. It's 8 p.m. and the sun has left Manhattan for better places. My big, serendipitous day has escaped like smoke.

Secondly, I have eighty-one unanswered text messages.

Did I mention I have anxiety? I scroll around and discover texts from all kinds of people. The wardrobe department wants my sizes and head-to-toe selfies. Production needs to know what kind of rental car I want. The Second A.D. needs more contract info. Production coordinator sends an enormous document that I must fill out. Covid department needs me to test tomorrow. The travel head wants my first born.

Also, Aurora texted me a few times.

The other sixty-four text messages are from a group text with the name "Frankenstein Stuntarinos" at the top. There are twelve phone numbers in it, and aside from Ed Fury and his assistant Jin Hoon (a rat-like, EDM-blasting martial arts dude in a backwards hat), I don't know any of them. I'm entering Barbaric Fury too quickly. A wind is shoving me in.

My phone buzzes in my hand. I've just been sent an updated version of the script.

Not yet ready to get off the floor, I call Aurora. She asks me how it went last night, and I tell her I honestly can't remember. She hesitates, and then asks, "How did you get home?"

"Aurora," I pant. "Listen. I just booked a gig. It's a big one. Three months in New Orleans."

"Wow!" she says. "Are you going to bring Wolfblood?"

"Um, I hadn't thought of that." I try to relax, inhaling deeply and rolling onto my side. Glass cuts my elbow, and more blood comes. I close my eyes. "Probably not," I say. "I'll be working long days." Dominican music starts thumping outside my window, accompanied by the sounds of happy voices buzzed after dinner, the usual reggaeton sunset party in Spanish. "I don't know what I'm gonna do," I say.

"Do you want to stay at my place for three months? Take care of Bloody? She has medicine that she needs for her—" but I don't finish.

Aurora exuberantly agrees, explaining that Jake has been stressed out about his tarot cards. Their apartment is a mess, and she wants to give him space to work. I thank Aurora, forcing myself to stand up and go to the kitchen for a Xanax and an Imodium and a banana.

Eventually, my nervousness reverses, and I'm in the clear. The pain in my stomach is better, my hangover reduced to mild nausea and sluggishness, so I crack open a beer and set to work on emailing everyone on the *Frankenstein* production team while kneeling at the side of my bed.

I don't look at the "Frankenstein Stuntarinos" text thread because it's too crazy.

OK—I glance at it, but nothing's important. Mostly jokes. They all know each other, or most of them do.

Wolfblood enters the room, looking like a mangey cartoon dumpster cat and sits on my ankles while I pray beside the bed. She purrs loudly until I get drowsy. By now it's 11 p.m. and my back isn't any better. The laptop is closed on the bed, and my face is buried dangerously in the comforter. I look like a dead, three-hundred-pound child.

If I die before I wake,
I pray the cat my feet to eat.

I can't lift my head.

Bubbles of light appear behind my eyelids, as I realize I'm suffocating. The bubbles become splotches of blue and aquamarine, now comets streaking all over the place. I manage to get my hands into fists under my face, allowing a small amount of oxygen to find my mouth. Wolfblood is sitting on the back of my head, trying to smother me. I shudder at the image, not seeing the humor which would be obvious to anyone who might be watching. I know without turning my head that my window curtains are open, and since my lights are on and I live on the second floor, anyone can look in and see a cat sitting on top of a corpse for what might have been hours.

I fall back asleep.

At some point in the night, there's a loud thud against my door. Someone has been knocking for a while, quietly at first, then louder. Now someone is yelling, something about the police department and the fire department.

I wake up fast, defibrillated with fear. Wolfblood tumbles off my shoulders in a flurry of scratches. Climbing to my feet, I take two steps toward the door before my back retaliates in full wrath. I have to stop.

Wolfblood faces the door, sitting an inch away from it, looking straight up. Her tail switches expectantly.

A large, heavy tool bag hits the floor behind my door, and an uppity voice says, "Alright, open it."

I almost make it to the door when the explosion goes off. My doorknob clangs to the floor, lock and cylinder scattering horribly.

Five people in uniforms are staring at me. Two cops, one fireman, and two paramedics. I can tell from their facial expressions that it reeks in my apartment.

I must be dreaming.

Wolfblood seems to have disintegrated. This is my first clear thought, probably because my door is open. Then I realize that I don't have a door anymore, just a metal flap in the wall, welcoming all of Harlem into my apartment to party. It's also letting the air conditioning out, which makes me nervous. This is followed by a more immediate fear when I realize there are drugs everywhere.

All these things cross my mind before I understand what's really happening. The fireman and EMS responders rush past me into the bedroom. The two cops lunge at me and start yelling. They shove me to the floor, and suddenly I feel like I've been hit by a grenade. My hearing fades, then slowly regains itself, while I lie pinned on my stomach. They're all talking about a body, looking everywhere for it. A knee lands in my middle back, which causes me to scream, and cold steel handcuffs bite into my wrists.

"What in the fuck is happening!" I yell. But before I can finish, there's another knee on the back of my neck, and the comets and splotches come back, smearing my vision, and I'm out.

Someone is shaking me. No, a lot of people are shaking me. My head and shoulders are strapped to a stretcher. I'm in an ambulance, the sounds of metal and plastic clattering around me.

A man is speaking. I can't hear what he's saying because it's swirled into the atmosphere. It sounds like the opening track on some metal album. Eventually a phrase emerges through the chaos. "Ah, there he is. Can you hear me? Did you hear what I just said?" It's one of the paramedics. He's sitting beside me, shining a pen light in my face, his other hand holding a notebook.

"Yeah," I mumble, even though I hadn't.

"No, you didn't," someone else says. I look down toward my feet. One of the cops is sitting by the rear doors of the ambulance like a guard. He's a black man, about my age, hair graying at his temples. "Man, you scared half the neighborhood. We got, like, eighteen complaints about you."

I'm realizing that my wrists are chained to the stretcher, and I'm having trouble breathing.

"Man, tell me you remember *something*," the cop says. He's smiling at me, holding his cellphone in his lap. I don't like his face. It knows too much. I want to kick it. I want my apartment. And my painkillers, and my cat. This sucks. A nasal canula is plugged into my nose, attached to an oxygen tank.

"What the hell is going on," I manage to say. Then I sneeze really hard, and my back rips apart horizontally. I shout something that sounds like *"jam!"* and both men recoil as if I attacked them. "I need a glass of water," I say. "Please."

"Mr. Mercier, you're under arrest—"

"For what?" I ask, before he can tell me.

The cop looks patiently at the paramedic, then back at me. "Mr. Mercier," he says, "pending further investigation, you're under arrest for possession."

THE STUNTED MAN

POSSESSION

"POSSESSION!?" I yell, and then scoff. "Well, why the hell am I in an ambulance? I need an exorcist! Look, can you call Jake? My front door is wide open."

I can hear my insides grinding like a garbage disposal. The cop speaks calmly to me, but I sense that he's full of coffee, ready at a moment's impulse to leap out of his skin like a thunderbird and save the world.

"Now, who's Jake?" he asks. "Is that the man who was in your apartment last night?"

"Jake isn't . . . nobody." I close my eyes, blotting out the two men and all the medical junk rattling around me. I think about Halona. There's something I'm not understanding here. Did something happen to her? I remember looking up at her apartment building from the outside, all Essex Street redux, with superimposed Thai restaurants and buildings that looked Botox-ed somehow. I remember nothing else. Is she OK? Is she hurt? Did they find my semen on her, and suspect me of—

These thoughts drop away, and I think, *Shit. Do I love her?*

Then I realize what the cop just said. The other thing.

The man who was in your apartment last night.

There was no man. Only me. No one but a hollow, burnt-out husk with an engine that won't quit.

"Mr. Mercier, we received multiple reports about a dead body in your apartment last night. We have photos, and many witnesses."

"No way," I chuckle, but it comes out sounding fake.

"They said they saw you clearly, and you looked dead." The cop pulls a small notepad from his utility belt and riffles through it, grinning. "Let's see here," he says. "His face was blue, his fingers were bent all crooked, and they didn't move for hours."

"I was drunk!" I cry, and the silence that follows feels like I just admitted something. "Look, I need water, please." The paramedic tips a bottle of water into my mouth, and I drink. Feeling a little better, I say, "Don't you think I would've woken up if I had been asphyxiating in the night?"

"Not with the kind of drugs you had lying around," the paramedic says.

"Then why am I here?"

"A couple of reasons," the cop answers. "We have questions regarding the drugs. And the photos."

"We also want to keep you safe for the night," the paramedic adds.

"It's morning already," I say. "What happened to my door? And my cat? I don't feel safe without my cat."

After a pause, the paramedic continues. "We've alerted your superintendent about the door. He said he'll have it fixed."

I sneeze again, harder this time. "Oh, that makes me feel really great."

"Now, listen," the cop continues. "The man in the photos, Mr. Mercier, is clearly you."

"That's what I'm saying!" I shout. "Everybody knows who I am!"

Another silence, during which the two men give each other an important glance. *Jesus, is there any word in the English language that isn't self-incriminating?*

Slowly, as if speaking to a child, the cop says, "Now why would everybody know who you are, Mr. Mercier?"

"Hey, what's your name?" I say. "You keep saying my name. I assume you've read me my rights. What's your damn name, *officer?*"

The black man on the tiny seat with the cheap blue NYPD uniform says, "I'm Officer Evans. This here is William. He's a paramedic."

"Why are you smiling?" I sneeze. "And why do I keep sneezing? Did you guys give me Narcan?"

"Yes," they both say.

Chilling silence, filled with plastic rattling.

Officer Evans says, "Now, let me ask you again. Why would everyone in the neighborhood know who you are? Do you sell them something?"

"We found a lot of drugs in your apartment," the paramedic says. "They were all around you."

"My cat," I say.

"You mind telling us why you have such a rainbow of Skittles in your apartment?"

I look at Evans totally soberly and say, "Not my child," then return my gaze to the ceiling. If you've never been in an ambulance bay, there's a lot of weird machinery on the ceiling. I've been in a dozen ambulances, but I have no idea what all that shit on the ceiling is.

It's still dark outside, only the feeblest pre-dawn light showing through the window. I get nervous when the sun is this weak. Manhattan is like a cool, crisp bedsheet about to get crumpled and sweaty and dirty.

"Why does everyone know who you are, Mr. Mercier?" the cop says. I've forgotten his name. I'll call him "Polestick" from now on.

"Because," I say, "I'm a three-hundred-pound, tatted-up white dude in the middle of Harlem!"

Polestick looks hurriedly at the paramedic. "We don't discriminate," he says. His writing pad, a pocket-sized flippy thing, is jouncing on his lap. "So," he says, jolting his gaze back to me. "What *do* you remember from last night?"

Pause. Plastic rattling.

"Mister Mercier?"

"I remember nothing," I pout. "Nothing credible. Not right now." A thought occurs to me. "I remember that I need a lawyer."

We're pulling into a hospital roundabout, grey and severe, dead-looking. The ambulance stops, but nobody moves or does anything. I can't see much through the windows. From outside someone says, "Portal three is open, go ahead." And the ambulance starts moving again.

Officer Polestick says, "Mr. Mercier, do you have a brother?"

"Lawyer," I say. "My brother is Layne Mercier. He lives in Los Angeles. Why?"

"Does he look like you?"

"Not at all. And he never would've been in my apartment anyways. He has three kids with ADHD and other made-up shit, and he doesn't visit me."

"And as far as you can remember, you were the only person in your apartment last night."

"Besides you, yeah!" I shout. "I have a steel door and three locks and window iron, so yeah! It was just me!"

"That's OK. Calm down, Mr. Mercier. We just have some questions. We received multiple reports of a dead body seen through your bedroom window. Now, we didn't find a body—"

"I'm the body!"

Polestick lowers his voice to exaggerate his patience. "We didn't find a body, but what we *did* find was blood. And broken glass. And the shower curtain had been torn off."

The paramedic murmurs, *"Lots* of drugs and alcohol."

"Everywhere," Polestick agrees.

The world is pulling away again. I try to look up at the hospital and its windows. Another mind full of rooms, most of them dark.

Officer Polestick watches me. He looks as if he has something to say, but rather enjoys keeping it in. I realize I'm holding my breath, so I let it out. This aggravates my back. "Guys," I say. "I'm obviously fine."

The ambulance reverses, then stops. The doors pop open, and arms reach in. I snarl at them, hard. "Hold on!" I scream at all of them. "I have a *fucked up back!*"

They drag me feet-first out of the ambulance. "Mr. Mercier, listen up." Polestick is stepping out of the vehicle, assembling his various weapons. "Your neighbors saw you clearly through the window, and they were all certain that you Jimi Hendrix-ed yourself. We found vomit and blood everywhere, and broken things." He smiles. "We also found a cereal bowl full of cat food, with a knife and fork in it."

"That's not true—"

"We're going to have you evaluated by a state official. Then we'll set you up with an attorney, and take it from there." Polestick slams the ambulance doors, and I'm wheeled, groaning through the Emergency Department's lower corridor.

ZOOM MEETING

I SPEND THE morning in a small emergency room with two other men. One of the men is asleep on a bed to my left. He smells like a rotting corpse, and he spasms sometimes. The other man is awake, but he doesn't seem to notice me. He's wiping his thighs and snapping his head around, grimacing, lost in whatever spectacle is playing in the theater of his mind. His meth days are all around him. His mind hotel is full of old misfits, all yelling and breaking lamps and spraying fire extinguishers. It's a cheap motel with thin walls, and no doors to compartmentalize, leaving the guests to scatter around at will. The man is overwhelmed. His mind is dark and full of terrors, squatters lurking in forgotten corners like shame.

The meth head has the most regrettable tattoos I've ever seen: an arm full of Pac-Man ghosts, a hand-drawn Nintendo 64 insignia, and a baby's face that's supposed to look realistic, but instead looks like some Cronenberg monster. The tattoos all scramble together, swarming like tattered thoughts as the man shimmies in his trance. He looks to be middle-aged like me, but skinny as a crack pipe. If I had my Klonopin, I'd give him two. Trying not to stare at him, nor the sleeping man who's now farting continuously, I close my eyes and realize I'm shaking. I take a few deep breaths to steady myself, and before long, I'm asleep.

In my dream, I'm not breathing. I'm back home, kneeling on the floor by my bed with my face buried in the comforter. Two men gently lift me up and lay me onto a narrow board. It's plastic and padded. Red lights flicker through the window, dashing shapes across my ceiling, and smells of plastic, iodine, and men consume me. The board I'm lying on floats backwards through my apartment. The sound of something rubber drags along the floor, maybe a locked wheel, or a sliding piece of equipment. I want to call out *"Bloody,"* but I can't open my mouth, and my mind is somewhere large and very far away.

Everything is more or less serene, until I realize I'm still not breathing.

I wake up with a gasp. The two drunk men are gone from the room, and now there's a new person here. He's lying where the meth addict had been when I fell asleep. This guy's also black, and he's dancing the same way, trying to wiggle out of his skin. But he's ten years younger than the other guy and has no tattoos, abysmal or otherwise.

I'm given a public defender who looks like a homeless George Clooney. I won't bore you with all the lawyer stuff. The cops painted guilt all over me. I received my psych evaluation, and of course I passed, so I was ultimately charged with a possession misdemeanor and a fine for public indecency. Apparently, acting dead while your cat sleeps on your head with your curtains open is illegal. My cellphone was eventually returned to me, and I was asked to leave the building.

One hundred and eighty-four text messages and seven missed calls, three of which are from Ed Fury, which alerts me that I'm in trouble—an absurd reaction, because I haven't done anything wrong. Either way, I won't check my messages until I get home, because I need a little drink first.

It's only one mile to my apartment, and the air is nice. A walk would do me some good. It's a warm clear day, and I need to think. Also, it might help loosen my back.

I call my superintendent, and he tells me that my door is already fixed. It was just a lock plate and a doorknob, and he had an extra one in his office. The other two locks were not broken, because they hadn't been latched when the break-in occurred. He tells me that I owe him bigtime, and I can tell from his tone, as well as the fifteen text messages he left me that that "simple" lock plate has ruined his entire week.

I don't call Aurora or Jake because I'm too embarrassed.

I find myself in the seedy part of Morningside Heights, forgetting that the park on 145th St. is set on a cliff that's unscalable, so I'm forced to backtrack to 149th St. where there's a staircase.

When I get to the staircase, I see a homeless man in the street. He's trying to get to the stairs so he can sit down, but his pants are coming off, and he's not wearing underwear, and he doesn't have enough strength to walk or pull up his pants.

As I get closer it becomes apparent that he's old, perhaps elderly. But what's most clear is that he's blotto drunk and needs help.

"Hey," I say. My three-hundred-pound shadow eclipses him. "You OK, sir?"

He mumbles something that I can't understand, but he doesn't have to explain the obvious trouble he's in. Cars roar past us on Bradhurst Avenue, blurring downtown in vengeful streaks. It's mid-afternoon, and the city is a river of noise, fire hydrants blasting water, kids out of school screaming, boom boxes, car horns, megaphones droning on about politicians in Spanish.

"Let's get you off the street," I say, looking around to see if this is a trick. It doesn't appear to be, so I turn back to the old man and take him by the arm. "Come on, buddy."

"Thank you, sir. I'll sit down." He's trying to walk but failing. He's looking down at his faded jeans which are dropping off, and his soft arms are limp. I help him take a few steps while he holds his pants around his knees. A kid grazes us on his bicycle without giving so much as a glance. A bird lands on the stairs like it's the easiest thing in the world. We get a couple of steps farther, and the old man throws his arms up in an alarming gesture, which causes me to step away from him. He topples over, now forfeiting his effort, and I rush in and catch him in my arms. But my back is swarmed with demons, so we both tumble into the grass, about ten feet from the stairs.

My adrenaline kicks in, sitting me upright. The old man has rolled onto his back. He gestures to the stairs with one hand—his version of up—and he's smiling, but not because he's happy. He looks at me with strangely clear eyes, and his smile says, *"If you weren't here, I'd be dead."*

He tries to pull his pants up, but they're tangled around his ankles, so I do it for him. His grayish brown penis is very close to my face, smelling like corn oil. Thankfully, the man helps me as the pants get closer to his hips. I do his belt.

We climb clumsily to standing. I don't know who's more crippled.

We have to get this man to the stairs. We have to find him something sugary to drink, some orange juice, in case he's a diabetic. Then we have to get ourselves home to our medicine cabinet and fuck-all. Then respond to a thousand phone calls. I haven't even checked my email since . . . how long has it been since Fury texted me and my life went to hell?

It occurs to me that I should also check in with the "Frankenstein Stuntarinos" text thread.

I get the man around the waist and gently limp with him over to the stairs. I think eighty people stepped around us.

When we get to the stairway, I check his pants. They're still good. He smiles at me gratefully, but I wonder if it's a bit routine. Raising my head to gaze up the length of the stairs, a vivid blue sky arches over us, the color of every beautiful day I've ever had.

"You diabetic?" I say.

He shakes his head.

"On any medication?"

He shrugs and makes a "psssh" sound.

"Take it easy, old man." I pat him on the shoulder. "Stay off the brown stuff."

There's a floorboard missing in my living room. Well, it's not missing, exactly. It's lying a few feet away from where it should be. And it's not a floorboard per se, but a plastic linoleum slat that Wolfblood must've clawed out of the floor when the fire brigade and all of them showed up.

I bring a cold beer into the bathroom so I can take an Imodium and a Valium. On my way to the bathroom, I chuckle to myself, remembering how that cop said he wanted to "keep me safe," but then left all the booze in my kitchen.

The smell in the bathroom is horrible, but I can't clean it up right away, because when I see the hallway floor my balls climb up into my stomach and I freeze.

A thin blue streak trails from my bedroom toward the front door. This causes my whole body to tingle, as the formless unreality of what I'm seeing begins to take shape. The blue streak is clearly the scuff of a small wheel—

A stretcher.

But it can't be a stretcher. There never was a stretcher inside the apartment.

So, I close the curtains in the bedroom and lie down on my bed.

The elaborate hotel / convention center / ballroom that is my mind is glistening. There's no other word for it. It's cavernous, gold, and glistening. As I float across the lobby—

The phone in my hand buzzes, and for an absurd moment I think it's Wolfblood calling. Then I wake up in horror, realizing that today is Wednesday, and I have a Zoom meeting with the Frankenstein people at some point.

It's 5 p.m. already. A pang of regret numbs my stomach. I remember the psychologist who drove up to Mount Sinai to evaluate me. She had to wait twelve hours for my blood toxicity levels to flatten out before she could give me my psych exam. Apparently, my blood toxicity had been twenty-five times the value of inebriation when I arrived that morning. This causes me to realize that I had been in the hospital for two nights, not one.

I scramble into the bathroom and take a quick shower, neglecting to reattach the shower curtain, and further splattering my bathroom with stink and soap.

I brush my hair and tie it up in a ponytail, then dry my beard as I begin checking all the correspondences on my phone. I haven't missed the Zoom meeting, thankfully. But Ed Fury needs to speak with me now, before the meeting begins.

When he answers his phone, I don't have time to explain my disappearance before he goes into a rapid-fire pep talk. He explains that at no point during the meeting am I allowed to speak, especially to Mr. Schilling. My job is to watch, unless I'm asked a direct question, in which case I'm to keep my answer short. Two cents, and not a penny more. I completely agree. This is when I notice a full bottle of red wine on the floor that I had opened at some point but never drank. It lies on its side by the nightstand, corked. I have nine minutes to drink that wine before the meeting starts, so I'll have to forego the rest of the emails, the "Frankenstein Stuntarinos" text thread that now has two hundred ninety-six unread messages in it, the two updated scripts I haven't opened, the sixteen texts from Aurora, one text from Jake, a voicemail from my mother who is probably intuiting something, and most importantly, hovering over everything like a flying saucer, the most important thing in town: a text from Halona.

On my laptop, the space behind me is clean and professional. Red string lights float above my piano which is adorned with black candles, portraits of myself in zombie makeup, a large hardcover display of H.P. Lovecraft's "Tales of Horror," and an actual-size life-cast of my head from the *Zombieland* movie.

I throw on a red blazer to appear even more Hollywood. Then I shuck the blazer, throw on a black leather jacket and sunglasses instead, take a slow, steadying breath, followed by a hit of cocaine, and open the Zoom link.

I'm the first person to arrive in the virtual space, and I congratulate myself on how smoothly everything has gone in the last two days.

I also assure myself that Wolfblood is close by, somewhere in the building, and she'll come home as soon as she's hungry.

Movie executives appear on the screen. At first, they're befuddled, as the internet connections finish sniffing each other out. But soon the image clears, and the executives' demeanors quickly right themselves. They're in the war room, sitting at a large table surrounded by images of various locations, art design mockups, wardrobe ideas and actors' head shots. They're all facing the front of the room where I imagine an image of myself is plastered on a giant TV screen or projector. In a flash I'm insecure, suddenly under a magnifying glass. My apartment starts to fold in like a ribbon, but when a chorus of caffeinated producers all cheer "hello!" and "there he is!" and "alright!" I'm set at ease.

"Hi!" I say, smiling like I'm the bassist in the band. I don't say anything else, remembering Fury's pep talk.

A man sitting closest to the camera says, "Hello, Alex, it's good to meet you! I'm David Morley, the director of *Everyone's Frankenstein*. Behind me is Patricia the producer, and you know Ed Fury." He gestures across the table.

Fury is enormous, easily fifty pounds heavier than I remember. His tiny image on my laptop is all biceps and baseball cap.

"What's up, bro!" Fury gleams, and I can tell he's on something other than just caffeine and expectation.

"How are you, Fury?" I say.

David Morley continues. "So, we're just waiting on Mr. Schilling, here."

Mr. Schilling. I want to laugh. *Sounds like a high school teacher. His name is Ben Fucking Schilling, you twits.*

Patricia tells Morley that Mr. Schilling will be jumping on at any minute, which generates a round of nods and approvals.

Fury says to me, "I'm so glad you're on board with us, bro! This film is going to be fucking epic."

"It's real, man," I say.

Morley adds, "I can tell from your backdrop that you're the perfect man for this."

I blink a few times. "Thank you, sir. I'm big into horror."

A new rectangle appears on my screen, causing the other two images to shuffle. Ben Schilling's face stipples in. He's holding a Diet Coke, a copy of his script lying in front of him. I know, the image of an actor with a Diet Coke and a script is not very descriptive, but in the moment I kind of feel like I know the guy. His appearance fizzles in through the pixels, causing him to tower over one hundred films and stare straight at me. His eyes are dark, with severe bags under them. But they're not unattractive; he has a Neil Gaiman artsy look, sixty years old, salt and pepper hair that's been fashionably tousled, some tattoos on his arms. A plain white T-shirt reinforces his "no makeup" look.

"Hi guys," he says, a little shyly.

Everyone applauds, and when no one's looking at me, I take off my sunglasses.

The meeting is easy. Schilling spends twenty minutes talking about the physical movement of his character, making visual references to other films, like Sachiko from *Ringu,* and the contortionist woman from *Malevolent.* My replies are sterile and perfect and unspecific. I take a lot of notes, beginning to feel as if it's all some elaborate math equation that I'm here to solve. Eventually Schilling changes direction and talks with David Morley about scene work, addressing changes he'd like to make to the script. "Dr. Frankenstein's monster would never say 'but,' he would say *'however,'"* and, "would it be funny if at this point, I said such-and-such?" and it's all going well because now I'm drunk again, and nobody wants to hear from me anymore.

"Well, that went well!" David Morley eventually says, after Ben Schilling has left the meeting. "Alex, you're a man of few words, and I love it!"

I wave a hand. "Thanks."

Fury leans forward and says, "Alright, bro, let's chat tomorrow. Keep your phone on you. There's a chance we'll want to bring you out a little sooner."

"Sounds good," I say.

They all thank me (profusely), and I click off.

I'm trembling, worried about Wolfblood, missing that sweet, ragged bag of fur. I lower my head, though not very much, because of my back. There's a wine bottle in my hand that I don't remember putting there.

Two seconds before I despair, a high-pitched sound causes me to stand up fast. This makes me cough, which sends a juggernaut crashing into my back.

I start to scream, but I haven't stopped coughing yet, so I spin around and convulse subtly, propping my back straight against the wall. There's a thud, and the room shakes. My heart, however, is full, and warm ripples of assuredness flow through my body like morphine, because the sound I'm hearing is a faint, fair-weather meowing.

Wolfblood's at the door. My Warrior Princess returns.

I waddle slowly to the door and let her in. She squeaks, and her tail waves like a tiny flag as she headbutts my shin as hard as she can.

Wolfblood is finally home. The Zoom meeting went well, and my affairs are more or less in order. Everything is now perfect.

And Halona texted me twice!

Before I check Halona's texts, I try to remember what happened the other night. Maybe more details will trickle in if I let them.

They don't, and I'm starting to think that maybe I didn't have sex with her, that the image of myself grabbing her hair was just a blind vision. Surely, I would've remembered something about the inside of her apartment, her bathroom, *something*.

I decide here and now: I am going to quit drinking.

Halona's first message says, *"Hi, hun!"*

Her second message, the next day says, *"I'm thinking about you in a Spider-Man costume, touching myself."*

I text her back, *"Hey babe! Sorry for the delay, I've been working."*

Then I open the group text. "Frankenstein Stuntarinos."

Three hundred and eighty-one messages, from a scroll of anonymous phone numbers. Most of them are gifs, and hearts, and annoying things of the like.

I have to scroll all the way to the beginning, but before I get there my intercom shrieks, sending goosebumps over my flesh like grassfire. My apartment dims for a second.

The cops! They're back!

My heart is slamming like a Slayer song as I struggle to inventory the apartment. Aside from the bathroom, everything looks OK.

I pad over to the front door, press the intercom button, and say, "Yeah."

Aurora brays, "Lex! What's up, it's me and Jake!"

I sigh, deflated. I'd almost rather the cops. I buzz them in, unbolt the door, then scramble into the bathroom to straighten up. There's a short, quiet moment while I wipe up some stuff.

When I stick my head out of the bathroom, they're stepping into my apartment cautiously, looking small, afraid of what they expect.

Jake says, "Dude, you got a new door."

"Yeah," I say. "The old one was broken."

"Sweet," he says, looking around.

"How are you doing?" Aurora asks, her eyes enormous.

"I'm fine, you know. Just busy." There's a pause. "I got a new gig."

After a moment, during which I analyze their facial expressions, I add, "Why did you guys just come over without texting?"

Jake answers while he straightens a picture frame on my wall. "Dude, we know how you get. We didn't want you ghosting us." This actually makes sense. I'm surprised it doesn't happen more often.

"We're just checking in," Aurora says, scratching her arm and staring at me.

I've always loved the way emotions pass over Aurora's face. It's like a constant procession. There's a rhythm to it. It's engaging, and it hurts me to see one expression remain on her face for so long.

"Well, thanks guys," I say. "I'm OK. Just tired."

Aurora continues, "Halona texted me. She said you were super fucked up the other night. You didn't want to sleep with her. You cried about your brother murdering some girl for like an hour, and you dropped your bike twice. She was worried about you."

"Why were you guys worried about me?" I ask. "Wait, Halona texted you?"

"Yeah, she found me on Facebook."

"Oh. OK."

My phone buzzes. It's Halona.

"Stunt work? Cool!"

"Why is everyone always up my ass?" I say to the room, and then I text Halona back quickly. *"Yeah, I was on location for two days. No cell service. Police drama. Cool shit. How r u?"*

Jake is talking. "Dude, did you see they're cutting down all the trees on Hamilton Place?"

I try to put my phone in my pocket, but I'm only wearing boxer shorts.

"Are you sure you're alright?" Aurora says.

I'm staring at nothing, completely frozen, phone dangling from my hand.

"Lex?"

Pause.

"Hello?"

"Yes, I'm fine!" I say a little too loudly, and I wiggle my arms to demonstrate.

They're looking at me like I just pissed in the punch bowl, and everyone saw me do it.

"OK," I say. "I might have gotten arrested, but that's all been settled now, and I feel good. Really good. There's no body."

They both flinch.

"I mean there's no *murder*," I quickly add. "Nothing happened. I was a little drunk, and the processing took longer than it should have. Everything's fine."

"You were in jail?" Aurora asks.

"Sweet!" Jake says.

"Yeah. It's not the first time," I say. "And it wasn't even real jail. It was hospital jail. Shit happens. No big deal."

A silence floats into the room and hovers. It's not until my phone buzzes that Aurora says, "What's this new gig you got?"

"Are you even sure you got it?" Jake adds.

"What's that supposed to mean, Jake? Is that a joke?" I'm fingering a mirror on the wall that somehow got cracked. "Are you condescending me? I'm a middle child, dude. I'm immune to that shit. I'm fucking *impervious.*" Then I add, a little softer, "Of course I got it."

"Well, what is it?"

I tell Aurora and Jake about the movie, and that I'm Ben Schilling's personal movement coach, and how my body sucks, and Ed Fury terrifies me, and I don't want to go. Then I plop onto the couch next to Wolfblood and stroke her fur, needfully.

"Let's go get a drink," Aurora says. She smiles and pats her leg. "Let's go celebrate your new job. And your, um . . . acquittal."

"I wasn't on trial, Aurora."

"Come on," Jake says. He's smoking a roach while walking out of my kitchen. I didn't see him light it. "You deserve this, dude. Let's honor the moment. Embrace the present." Then, looking down, he adds, "Your floorboard is ruined."

"Is that *blood?*" Aurora's pointing at the floor.

There's a silence, and inside it I see that Jake and Aurora are hooked, and nothing can make them stop loving me. Not tonight at least. A pillow is on my floor. It's smashed and misshapen, lying too still.

Finally, I say, "Somewhere close by. I'm not going downtown."

THE STUNTED MAN

REPORTAGE

HARLEM PUBLIC, AKA "Jake's Place," is a mostly white-people bar with loud pop music and nonexistent greetings, and men wearing shirts that say "EQUALITY," and "BIG GUNS, SMALL DICKS," and "KEEP CALM AND STOP ASIAN HATE," all in sans serif text like subtitles under their necks. One woman walks across the room without looking at anyone, wearing a shirt with a large uterus printed on it. She trips on a chair and spills her drink on a young man wearing suspenders and says, "Sorry, person," and then saunters away indifferently. This is where Jake wants me to work.

We sit down at an overly lacquered table. Jake and Aurora seem fixated on me. *When do you leave? Is your back feeling better? How long is the gig?*

I don't want to talk about myself. I ask Jake why he wanted to come to his beatnik hipster bar, and he tells me he loves this place, and they make great Old Fashioneds. I suggest he tries *enjoying* whiskey instead, but he just looks at me and says, "What, like you?"

A glum-looking guy in a trucker hat and a T-shirt that says, "HATE WON'T MAKE US GREAT" is looking at me. I feel like everyone is silently screaming at one another. Arcade Fire's new album segues into Post Malone, which causes me to close my eyes and think about the ocean. I'm tired of this whole fucking quagmire.

Halona texts me again. But before I can read it, she's knocked swiftly aside by a text from Ed Fury.

"Hey bro, can you come out on Friday?"

I text him back, *"Yes, sir!"*

Jake's voice cuts through the noise. "Dude, they're cutting down all the trees on your street! What's that about?"

Through the window, the planted trees, skinny and meek, seem somehow essential. They entertain the squirrels, at the very least. I pity those squirrels. They always scamper up the trees when I start my Harley. I love that.

"Lex," Jake says, and whatever he says after that disappears while I'm thinking about leaving Harlem in two days, clenching and unclenching my fists. My body is in the worst condition it's ever been in.

"I'm going to get another drink," I say firmly, and I chug my entire IPA, wipe my beard with a hand and eject myself from the table.

A young man with a beehive hairdo and horn-rimmed glasses is tending the bar. He recognizes me from the subway platform and smiles. "What'll it be, friend?"

"Pretty miserable," I reply. "IPA, please."

"Hazy?" he hopes.

"No, the other kind, please."

He turns to draw me a beer and the back of his shirt reads, "NO GENDER PRONOUN, NO SERVICE." And finally reconciling my back pain, a smile loosens on my face, welcoming the fact that I'm leaving New York, maybe forever. Things start to fold together. New Orleans is full of music and flowers and oysters, and my life here isn't that great anyways.

The bartender hands me my beer, and I pay him thirteen dollars, then raise it up to my lips and take a long drink. "That's a great beer," I say, grinning.

The bartender looks at me.

"Mosaic forward. Pillowy mouth feel. Is it local?"

The bartender agrees with me, so I turn around and lean against the high lacquered ledge, casually scanning the room for babes, not really caring. The overly lit bar tries to consume me.

Soon the lights dim, and the music style changes. Dinner is over. Aurora is talking like herself again, relaxed, sometimes eyeing me as a mother would her child, as I tumble around using my momentum to keep the vibes flowing. Jake is also looking at me, half spiritually, half not.

I brought a half gram of coke with me because there's a drug dealer on every floor of my building, and I think about that now.

The night pursues as usual. We move to Morocco, a club on Broadway, because Jake brought it up, and it's close to my apartment.

A scrawny guy at the entrance stands next to the bouncer holding a fake multicolored shotgun, and he's aiming it at people who walk past the club on Broadway, compulsively yelling, *"bam! bam!"* They're underneath a zebra-striped marquis, and I don't know what time it is, but I'm ducking from this guy's shotgun while Aurora clutches my arm. At first, we pass the club, catch our breath, then we go back and enter.

We slip right, through a doorway and up the stairs where there's a dance floor and loud music. A young couple glides past us at the top of the stairwell—a black boy and a white boy—and the black boy is yelling about how he doesn't remember how to cut up the cocaine out of the bag. "It's so *sticky*," I hear him cry.

I text Halona and invite her to join us. She declines, explaining that she's a physical therapist, and she has an appointment in the morning. I feel bad because I never asked her what she does for a living, despite telling her every miserable detail of my own life.

When we arrive at the dance floor, I get a stupid idea.

Without thinking, I grab Jake and tango-walk him backwards onto the dance floor. The crowd, which is mostly gay because Morocco is a gay club, turns toward us with slow, supplicating awareness.

Jake and I are a grinning whirlwind, our presence an ocean storm. I am death metal, clad in red, the devil himself, dancing flamenco. The crowd notices us and starts screaming. Aurora is laughing, and my back is strong again.

I remember going on my toes, steel-tipped motorcycle boots, and spinning on them. I remember being pleased. There was a time when I could do five pirouettes, pretty much consistently, but nowadays it's like three. Tonight, I did two. Clean, effortless double pirouettes, lilting at the end like a flame.

At the end of our dance, I jump off the balcony. There's a swimming pool on the first floor. I splash into it crazily, but it's only four feet deep, and I hit the bottom hard. A security guard ushers me out of the club, while Aurora scrambles around us, pleading, "He's a professional stuntman! It's OK, he's a *stuntman!*"

Now I'm back home, and I'm moving around doing stuff repeatedly. I finish the half gram of coke. Wolfblood wiggles past me, and I try to scoop her up, but I miss. She swishes off like a fish into the kitchen.

Eight a.m. is when I always wake up, even on binges. Tomorrow is the only day I can get anything done, so after a while I put myself to sleep. My head is full of ambitions.

Eight a.m., and my body is hard cement. It's impossible to move, but it feels great, so I sleep some more.

Nine a.m., and I'm still obdurate, so I sleep some more, whole body tingling with pleasure.

Ten a.m., and I'm practically paralyzed. But I'm happy with my decision, so at 10:18 I slowly writhe out of bed.

If I had died at 10:17 in an earthquake, I would've died peacefully.

STAY OUT OF NEW ORLEANS

MY FLIGHT LEAVES tomorrow morning.

After double-checking with Aurora about Wolfblood, I log on to Amazon and order thirty pounds of cat food and seventy pounds of cat litter. I'm almost out of drugs because the cops took most of them, but there are still some old pill bottles under my sink. Some kind of painkillers, I can't remember. The labels are all worn out, but I believe they were good pills, pleasant in a gloomy, enveloping sort of way.

I'm able to score a half gram of coke, this time from the fourth floor.

I visit a Duane Reade pharmacy because I need Christmas lights, and some new furry slippers for the hotel. Then I pick up six bottles of CBD from the weed store.

Somewhere in the afternoon, after my Covid test at the Universal Building in Columbus Circle, I have to take a break in Central Park to smoke a joint.

A woman is sunbathing on a grassy slope. Above her is the street and the enormous towers of Columbus Circle. A Whole Foods Market the size of the Vatican. Her eyes are closed, headphones in, and she's lying on her back. In the patch of green surrounding her, a blackbird stands arrogantly by her head. It's eating something in the grass, and from my angle, with one eye squinted closed, it looks like the bird is perched on the woman's forehead and pecking at her face.

I approve.

I think about Ed Fury. There's something about me he doesn't understand.

Ed Fury can't appreciate that where I come from is underground, down where the worms and beetles squirm. Down where the drums rumble. Where I'm from, there's nothing to do but guitar solo. Ed Fury doesn't understand that.

The friend I lent my harness to meets me in the park. He's bigger than me—an actual three hundred, not a cynical two-eighty. The soles of his shoes are squashed like slices of white bread. He hands me my harness and says, "Bro, I need to get a mouthguard."

I stub out the joint and say, "Yeah."

I decide that I'm not going to leave by way of the fire escape like I did last time. That was ten years ago, and I fucked up my ankle doing it. Instead, I'm going to gather my things peacefully and take the elevator down.

Wolfblood's fur is the most beautiful I have ever seen it. Despite her old, fuzzy clumps she's radiating, my soul apart from my body. The pain I feel is physical, right in the center of my chest. It burns and whispers, and cries mournfully from Wolfblood's soul: *No. Please don't go.*

Pulling myself away from Bloody is the only hard part about leaving. It feels counterintuitive. She's sixteen years old and looks like Keith Richards, ruddy-eyed and exhausted. Most of her facial markings have been worn away, rendering her a dull unflashy grey. Time is a river, and it washes all the color out of us.

"Bloody," I say, sitting on the floor with her, suitcases clumped together by the door. I'm petting her while crying, and she's purring loudly despite the knowledge that I'm leaving without her. My beard is salty and wet. "Bloody. You be a good little baby. I'll be home soon. Look at your face. Look at your *molecules*. Look at your beautiful face."

I lean in to kiss her face, but she pulls her head back a mile and a half, the way only cats can do.

I knew when I adopted Wolfblood from the Korean market that I signed a contract with God for a twenty-year run. But the devil was there too. He handed me the pen, because when God takes Wolfblood back in twenty years, the devil will be there to hold my head and force me to watch.

Before the car service arrives, I take an Omeprazole for my stomach. Then in the car, before we arrive at LaGuardia, I take an Oxymorphone for the pain.

I glide through security like a floating block of ice and make it to my gate with over an hour to spare.

At the bar—some knockoff Hard Rock Café—Stevie Nicks is playing, but they don't have any craft beer, so I order a twenty-two-ounce Sam Adams and think about Halona. Aurora won't show up at my apartment until tomorrow, and I don't want to think about Wolfblood all alone. So, I reminisce on how small and precious Halona is, and how many opportunities I tend to miss because of my drinking, and where those opportunities might have led. Which leads me to the mystery of this gig. And spiritually, I wonder why I was hired while in the absolute lowest place possible. The highway of life is long and winding, with mountains in all directions. And here I am crouched in the ditch, alone on the side of the road. And who pulls over to give me a ride? Ed Fury?

Where do people like me end up? All those years on the road, with nomadic artists and circus nuts. So many of them were drug users. So many broke their bodies. Life is about the journey, not the destination, sure. But we all have to wind up somewhere.

Last night I called an old friend I hadn't spoken to in years. His name is Allen, a brogue American acrobat I toured with in Cirque du Soleil, fifteen years ago. I asked him what he was up to these days. Allen is four years older than me. Fifty, fuck me sideways.

Allen said that he was mowing lawns at his kid's high school. "Technically, I'm a groundskeeper," he said, with so much regret he sounded physically pained to tell me this. "But all I do is drive a lawnmower around the football field and baseball diamond."

"That's not bad," I said, and I meant it. Most days I would settle for anything to stop performing.

When I asked Allen how his wife was doing, he said that she had left him. She wanted him to stop using drugs and drinking so much, but he hadn't. So now he keeps grounds for the school's athletic department, somewhere in Indiana. And in turn his daughter can attend private school on pretty much full scholarship. He still uses drugs, and was using them while on the phone with me.

I've had conversations like this with too many friends from my past. I'm continually upset by them. These men were world-class performers, the crème de la crème, and it saddens me to learn that the people I looked up to—masters, *legends*—are now discarded like old, tattered legwarmers at the bottom of a lost-and-found box.

When I see Ed Fury on Monday, if my back isn't too bad, I'll give him a hug. And not a one-armed bro hug but a real, slow motion, movie ending hug.

Time is a river that deposits us places.

I sleep most of the flight. My dreams are wild and incongruent, rearranged like underground tunnels.

I won't go into details, but at one point my body had become a bank vault, my back a thick, rectangular steel door. A woman with fingers for teeth and boobs for arms was drilling into my back like some sloppy ghoulish safe cracker. Her head lolled from side to side as if to music, and she was grinning like a crackhead. Her drill whistled loudly in my ears, like an airplane ventilation system. When she breached the safe, my back broke open in a slow yawn, and she screeched, delighted, and stuck her boob arms inside me, drawing out a rickety paramedic stretcher piled atop with bundles of money. The stretcher had blue rubber wheels, and one of them was dragging, close and familiar, but recalling no specific memory.

When I wake up, there are thirty minutes left in the flight. So I put on a Ben Schilling movie, and wait to land.

New Orleans is broiling hot on my skin. I feel like a chicken in a gumbo. Despite the heat, the sky is a dark twilight grey, the air sweet and thick, like ozone and bay leaves.

A man I recognize from my flight walks outside next to me. He's carrying a toddler on his shoulders, and he says, "I ain't been this humid since frickin' North Carolina! Or frickin' . . . South Carolina!"

"Man," I say, "tell me about it."

As soon as I get in the Uber, the rain starts to fall. Holy Lucifer, it rains a lot in New York, but this is some next level shit. Fake horror movie rain, with thunder like mortar fire. Frankenstein lightning. I wish music could be like this. The car is trembling, but the driver doesn't seem to notice. "Let's see," he says, looking at his phone. "You're going to The Wollcroft Hotel?"

At first, I'm too shocked to respond.

How are we gonna shoot a movie in this?

Hopefully, very slowly.

"Yes, Wollcroft Hotel," I say. "Thank you." Sweat begins to creep out of my skin like worms.

The driver swishes into traffic like a pursuant shark.

I reach into my pocket for a fentanyl tablet. I don't like being a passenger in a car. I close my eyes and listen to the downpour as it widens into something abyssal. After enough time passes, maybe twenty minutes, I open my eyes. It's full dark outside, and there's music in the car. Sad New Orleans jazz leaks from the speakers, and the windows are crying. Incriminating red light bleeds everywhere, and we're high up on some elevated causeway, careening into downtown. There's a sports arena next to another, bigger sports arena. The Superdome, I assume. Beyond that, through the water-streaked glass, Atlantis.

"Are we almost there?" I say loudly, trying to be heard over the rain.

The driver looks at me in the rearview mirror and says, "Yessir. Five minutes."

"Is it always like this?"

"Like what, sir?"

"Like this! Like a film noir fucking afterbirth."

"Oh no, sir. N'awlins is a beautiful city." He gestures out the windshield with one hand. "Sunshine, music, beautiful women."

"What's wrong with this picture, then?" My mouth floods with a coppery taste, and I realize that I'm pulling on my beard a little too hard.

"It's just a storm," he says. "It'll pass in five minutes. She likes to wash herself. Wash away the dirt and what-not. She do this all the time. How she keep it beautiful."

"By turning into a Batman movie."

"Yessir!"

My first order of business is to buy a lot of shoes. My boots are already ruined.

The Uber driver continues. "You know, Miss N'awlins is choosy about who she lets in, and who she lets out. They shuttin' down the airport right now. You lucky. She must like you." The car hydroplanes for a second, causing my heart to splash so hard that my vision blurs. The driver yells, "Ah! Dang!" and continues driving serenely. "Carondelet, next exit," he says. "Almost there."

I'm holding onto my beard like it's a handrail on a runaway subway car. Slowly, I let go of it, then search for my phone to text Aurora and check on Wolfblood. For a terrified moment I can't find my phone, but then the fentanyl detonates inside my body, and the rain sounds like dogs barking, and I fall asleep.

"Sir!" the driver yells again. My eyes roll open one at a time. "Shit man, what's wrong with you!"

"Hey," I say. "Are we here?"

The driver is standing next to me with his hands on his hips. My door is open. He seems pissed, but it's obvious that he had been worried only a moment before, and the relief of discovering that I'm not dead and I never vomited is replaced with indignant victimization, as if I had played some kind of prank on him.

"Yes, we're here!" he says. "And so are the cops gonna be in like ten seconds! You been like this for five minutes!"

"Oh, damn," I hear myself say.

"Come on!" he shouts. "Get out of my car!"

I slide like concrete out of the car and climb to my feet, steadying myself with a hand on the trunk. The car is cherry red. I never knew that. The rain has stopped. Now there's only smoking streets and swaying trees. Air pockets like warm ghosts.

"Your bags are over there," he says, gesturing to my two suitcases: a massive OGIO stunt bag packed with gear, and a regular square Samsonite. I sigh. I don't deserve those bags. They're as bloated with bullshit as I am, standing like vagrants by the sliding glass doors in the night.

"Hey, thanks," I say, looking down, unconsciously checking my pockets. "What's your name?"

"Fuck you, man!" He gets in his car, then starts typing on his phone that's affixed to the dashboard.

I collect my suitcases, slog them around in a circle to face the sliding glass doors, and take a deep breath.

I have arrived. Home at last.

After patting my hair to make sure it isn't frizzing, I walk up to the sliding glass doors and slam my face into them, hard. It's louder than it should be, and it wakes me up.

"You gotta push the button!" the Uber driver shouts, as he peels away, carving a swirl of *Back to the Future* steam on the road behind him.

"Well, damn," I say to nobody. The front desk staff are laughing inside. I can hear them, but I can't see them.

I have no idea where I am. Convention Center District, downtown, or near downtown. All I know is that these front desk people are in for a busy three months. If the Wollcroft Hotel is a mind, it's about to go crazy. Certifiable, in fact. Bats in the bell tower, all that. I'm a little eccentric, sure, but the rest of the stunt team will overwhelm them. I've seen it before. We're stuntmen. We're going to wreck everything.

Just. You. Wait.

Miss Jenny checks me in, and she's so sweet I want to roll around in bed with her even though she weighs more than I do. She tells me a bunch of things about the hotel, and about the city while I sway and nod, and she seems amused, still giggling at me, and everything's fine.

She explains that due to the pandemic, room cleaning services are suspended, unless I request it beforehand through reception. "That's good," I say, and toss her a wink. She also tells me I have a rental car, and she shows me the key. I tell her to leave it at the front desk in case any of my colleagues want to use it, and she obliges.

Miss Jenny and I exchange a few laughs. She's more of a host than receptionist. I ask her if Room 666 is available, mostly just hoping for a room on the top floor, but she tells me there aren't sixty-six rooms on each floor, only twenty-six, and "today's your lucky day," because Room 626 is available and ready for occupancy. She asks me if I want one key or two. I say, "One, ma'am," and raise my eyebrows suggestively.

After I take my key, Miss Jenny tells me that I have nice eyes, which causes me to bark laughter, because I know my eyes are hollow, and yellow, with a dead milky film over them.

The Wollcroft is old, possibly eighteenth-century, which is rare for the Convention Center District. There are a few historic buildings in this area, but mostly recent developments. I'll come to find out later that the Wollcroft was built in 1801 by the French, and later invaded by the Americans as part of the dispersion of 1904, when the Americans pushed the French north into a "French Quarter." The hotel was originally named Le Castille, probably for its size and battlement shape, but was renamed in 1904 in honor of General Wollcroft who led the attack on the great stone building.

My walk to the elevator is long, along all three sides of the courtyard. There's a swimming pool in the courtyard, probably in the very place that old battle was fought. Death toll? Unknown. Enough blood to fill a swimming pool? Almost certainly. I'm walking slow-mo, steamrolling the carpet with three months of shit behind me.

What was that old, really good movie? *Hotel Transylvania.* The Wollcroft feels like a hotel for monsters. The next few months will be spent in an old, tower-like room with artificial movie monster makeup calked into every crevice. Makeup mostly removed but still in evidence, gray and purple behind my ears, lining my fingernails, tracing the corners of the sink and shower. We're only real monsters if we're being poetic.

I'm on the top floor. The hunchback in the bell tower.

Doze-walking to my room, the carpet slides thickly underneath my suitcases. It's adorned with purple shapes that crisscross in some pattern, but I can't tell if they're Spanish crosses or fleur-de-lis'.

I go up an old, trembling brass elevator to the sixth floor. My room is at the end.

Without opening any suitcases, without checking to see if I have a bathtub, I drop my cellphone and faceplant onto my bed, leaving all ninety-seven unanswered text messages to dry like paint on the floor.

I wake up shivering at some hour. My throat is dry and scratchy, but otherwise I'm feeling pretty good. My thermostat is set to sixty-four, so I adjust it to seventy-six, and check the bathroom to see if there's a tub. There isn't one, only a shower. But there is a kitchen with a full-size fridge, and that's good.

My back is feeling better, and it only takes thirty seconds to pick my phone up off the floor.

One hundred twenty-four text messages, including one from Halona.

Tomorrow, I have a nasal swab in the morning, and wardrobe fittings in the afternoon. Then I have Sunday off, and we start rehearsals on Monday.

A message from Aurora was sent ten minutes ago, with photos of Wolfblood looking happy and helpless in her lap.

Halona has sent me a photo of her breasts. They're small and look suspiciously like a child's breasts, but they turn me on, nonetheless.

I sit down on the bed and return the favor, pulling up my shirt and snapping a photo of my scar.

In the photo, my nipple is just off-center, showing an eleven-inch crooked scar underneath the thunderbird tattoo on my collar. The scar is nasty, shaped like a check mark but backwards. It's only two years old and still pink. In photos it shows up forwards sometimes, like a real check mark. Such a trip. A sarcastic verification of approval. I got that scar when a fire truck flipped and rolled over me on a movie called *Piranha: Undead*. It was an accident, totally unforeseen. The fire truck hit the curb and went sideways fast, rolling it, and there I was, supposed to jump out of the way, but the thing was too fast—just a wall of red blood rolling toward me like *The Shining*. It hit me square in the chest and went over me, knocking me out for four days. It also broke eight of my ribs and tore off my boots, with two of my toes still inside them.

A bible-length scroll of gifs and emojis on the ostentatious "Frankenstein Stuntarinos" text thread, which I've decided to stay off of, due to my social anxiety and the fact that I don't know how to make a gif.

I do know how to make a shower, so I go into the bathroom and turn on the water, as hot as possible. Then I go back on my phone and look up bookstores in New Orleans.

Steam creeps out of the bathroom like a CGI monster, as I come to discover that there are no traditional bookstores in the city of New Orleans, independent or otherwise. There is one Barnes and Noble twenty miles outside the city, and a few used bookshops that sell nonfiction, history books about brothels and voodoo and vampires.

My stomach rumbles as I step out of the shower. I grab my phone to look up what's good around here. I have oysters on the brain.

But instead, I find a new text from Ed Fury.

Hey, bro, did you get the call sheet?

I text him back, promptly, *No, sir.*

It's in the group text.

You put the call sheet in the middle of all those memes and jokes??

I delete this last text without sending it, then scroll through the Stuntarinos text thread until I find the call sheet and write back, *Got it, thanks!*

Now I can see who I'll be working with.

A bunch of people I don't know.

Halona texts me back.

Shiiiiiiit! You are scarred, dude!

In between my Covid brain-stabbing and my wardrobe fitting, I take myself to Frenchmen Street to soak up some vibes and hear some music.

I'm driving a black '22 Dodge Caravan with a kick-ass sound system. I'm able to park the minivan on the corner in front of a Willie's Chicken Shack, across Frenchmen Street from the local bookstore. I'm checking items off my to-do list before I've even had a beer. This is great.

Geaux Nowhere Books is a hole in the wall, and all their books are historical, biographical, or of local supernatural folklore. In one corner of the tiny room, the desk clerk is young and attractive, so I browse a little.

"What's good?" I ask, thoughtfully touching the spine of a book about the poet, Codrescu.

"Well, what are you into?" she says back.

"I like fiction," I say, turning my attention to an orange cat who's sleeping on a crate with a blanket in the corner. I start to walk toward it, then realize that what I just said might have been insulting. I didn't mean to imply that all this nonfiction literature is uninteresting. Sometimes I come off as upset, or entitled. "Or like, horror," I say. "Scary stuff. Ghost stories. There's a lot of cool stuff in here." I gesture around with a hand. The other hand is petting the cat.

"Yeah, this place is cool," she says. "Pretty dark, too." She doesn't stand up, but she leans forward and points to a bookshelf on the far wall. "I think I have something you'll like," she says. "Right there."

An old, leather-bound edition of *Dracula* sits in a glass case. The cover is tattooed with intricate stamp work, rounded at the corners from time.

"Nineteen oh-one," she says, smiling at me with her lips closed like a weirdo.

"Wow, thanks." I let go of the cat and walk towards her. "But I'm more of a *Frankenstein* guy. Know what I'm saying?" I put a hand on her desk.

"Frankenstein?" she says, confused.

"Yeah," I say. "Or like, whatever. I read *Dracula* pretty recently. Been doing the classics. It wasn't that good. *Frankenstein's* better."

The girl lowers her head doubtfully and thinks about this. After a moment, she looks back up at me, snaps her finger and says, "I have an idea."

"Oh yeah?" I say. "What's that?"

She points toward the door and says, "Stay out of New Orleans."

SHOWGIRLS

"WHAT?" I SQUEAK. "I thought we were vibing! Not everyone likes *Dracula*. It's so old, and—"

"No," she says. "*Look*." She's still pointing. *"Stay Out of New Orleans*. It's a book, and it's new, and it's fiction. You'll definitely like it." She's not pointing at the door, but next to the door. "Right there."

I turn around. Sure enough, there's a small bookshelf packed with fresh copies of the same book. They look as if they had been printed only minutes before. Green jackets, and the most impressive font I've ever seen.

"Stay Out of New Orleans," I mutter, verifying what the girl just told me. I walk over to the shelf and pick one off. "Foreword by Chris Rose. Shit, that's legit."

"Yeah," she says. "It's a really good book. It's all about the seedy parts of New Orleans, like, pre-Katrina. A lot of it takes place in the French Quarter. Super dingy, scary stories."

"No shit," I say. "This is perfect. Thank you."

"Quite welcome," she says.

I pay the nice lady, and as I turn to leave, she adds, "And just so you know, *Frankenstein* is a lot older than *Dracula.*"

I cross the street and toss the book into my minivan. Then I head up Frenchmen Street to see what's good. My feet feel good. My back feels pretty good.

I have a wardrobe fitting this afternoon, but I only have a day and a half left to drink Louisiana beer before I go completely sober for three months. List of breweries off the top of my head: Urban South, Parish, Great Raft, Abita, Gnarly Barley, Faubourg, Second Line.

Almost everything on Frenchmen Street is closed.

The Spotted Cat is open, and a slick, scraping Zydeco rhythm can be heard from the street. It's Creole, and it shuffles.

As I step inside the club, a clarinet tumbles ecstatically over everything. I sit down at the bar, blocking like eight people's view of the bandstand.

"What's good!" I shout. "What are we drinking?"

The bartender gives me narrow eyes, the kind reserved for tourists. "Sazerac," she says. "One?"

"Yeah, thanks," She slams a tiny napkin on the counter and walks away, grabbing a shaker from under the bar.

I wait. The Sazerac arrives, and it's delicious. Mint, licorice, whiskey, and sugar.

"This is great," I shout at the bartender. "What kind of local beer you got?" I gesture to the Sazerac. "The flavors don't have to match."

"Juicifer," she says.

"One please."

The jazz music prattles pleasantly like a big cat dancing on my face. The piano player next to me is entranced, just swatting the piano with both hands as if slapping it out of a fainting spell. He looks like a brilliant toddler, but he plays great. The band is unstoppable.

The Juicifer is excellent too, so I grab another one for the road and head back to the minivan, sipping the beer while I walk. Mossy oaks, large as cathedrals, hang over the cobblestone street, waving in the warm breeze.

My fitting happens. The wardrobe warehouse is attached to Stage C, which is the stunt gym. This is where we'll be together from here on out. Stage C, baby. Remember that.

A friendly, fashionable woman gives me some terrible outfits to try on, including a bright green beanie, a dorky neighborhood patrolman's uniform, and ultimately, to add insult to injury, some skinny jeans.

Humiliated now, but still grateful to have a job, I decide to hit the French Quarter. Hotel first. Gotta drop off the van. But after that, it's walking distances all night.

Now, you don't go to Bourbon Street to buy drugs, obviously. You go there to schmooze with the strippers and the bouncers, and to find out *where* to buy drugs. Historically, the tactic checks out. Trust your training. It's the first stop, which is better than the last stop, which of course is the bus station, looking for North African-looking guys lingering in the corners, either solo or in groups. But there's a fentanyl outbreak, and college kids are dying right and left, so we have to be careful. Prince and shit.

Floating pairs of young women in showgirls' outfits—thongs and headdresses and fishnets—wander around selling photo ops for tips. They're some of the more cheerful people cutting up Bourbon Street. One of these lavish duets notices me, smiles, and I kind of get a boner.

Damn, I'm not ready for this, I think. I scan the crowd and grimace. Signs of injury and recovery are everywhere. The crowd thickens. The two-story storefronts along Bourbon Street are narrowing, pushing me into the street. The balconies feel as if they're about to collapse.

I switch over to Royal Street, ducking into a dive bar on Toulouse for a Juicifer. You can drink on the street in New Orleans, because God loves the South.

Another pair of showgirls passes me on Royal. The taller one, a brunette with glasses points at me and says, "Hey, you want a photo?"

"Nah," I mumble, waving a hand, and I keep on walking. All those years in New York have made me slippery.

She calls after me, "You want to talk about one?"

"No thanks," I say over my shoulder. But then a few feet later I stop and pretend to look at my phone. These two girls are locals. They'll know where the party is.

After studying my phone for a minute, I look back at the two girls. They haven't gotten far. There are fewer people on Royal Street. Just the homeless, a few tourists, and some gallery owners.

I walk casually toward the showgirls.

"You having second thoughts about that photo?" the tall girl with the glasses smiles.

"I wouldn't mind talking about it." I'm running a hand through my beard that's exploding in the humidity.

"OK," she says. "Where are you visiting from?"

"The grave," I say.

We do the small talk, and they immediately warm up to me. When we run out of things to say, there's a pause.

"Hey," I say, tapping the toe of my boot on the cobblestone, buckles jangling nervously. "Do you girls happen to know where I could go *skiing* around here?"

The tall girl starts. Doubt flickers across her glasses. "Oh shit," she says. "Alabama . . . Lookout Mountain is less than four hours—"

"No, no, no," I say, holding up a hand. "I mean *skiing,* skiing."

I make the most trustworthy face I can put on believably and wait.

"Ooohh!" they both say, and the tall one continues. "Of course! You can call my friend Raj. He's great. He's a doctor, and he does the whole Ketamine thing to fight depression, and he always has the best stuff. He's great. Do you have WhatsApp?"

"Yeah," I say, putting my hand down. "I mean, I need to download it. But I have an account. Yeah."

"You have to use WhatsApp because it's encrypted," she says. "It's untraceable! You can text whatever you want."

"Totally," I pretend to agree. "What's his number?"

She gives me Raj's phone number and tells me to tell him that Jamie the Showgirl put us in touch. I download the app, hand Jamie ten bucks and start to walk away.

"Hey, how about that photo now," she says after my back is turned.

I stop. "I don't like how I look in photos. No thanks."

"Come on, you know you want one."

We make a compromise, and I take a picture of the two girls, without me in it. This way, I don't have to look at myself later.

I continue to tour the French Quarter while I wait for Raj to get back to me. I sample some more local suds, then eventually slog my way back to the Wollcroft.

Halona texts me.

Do you have any more scars? I love scars, there so masculine.

I text her a photo of my leg. A long keloid squirms up my inner thigh like a water snake. This one came from being thrown through a kitchen window, eight years ago. When I hit the floor the room shook, causing a meat cleaver to fall from a ceiling-mounted pan rack, and it was not a prop. This is why I don't work on student films anymore. An inch to the left and it would've been my femoral artery. Also, what's up with Los Angeles ex-pats knowing nothing about earth-quake safety? Who hangs a meat cleaver from the ceiling? Leatherface? No one's heard of earthquakes?

Daaaaang!!! Halona replies. *That's crazy!! How's the movie going?*

The last of my clothes come off, and I'm standing in the middle of my hotel room.

I haven't started yet, I write. *I'm prepping.*

My phone lights up with a notification from WhatsApp. The eagle of freedom has taken flight.

Raj: *1/8 shrooms $50. Powder shroom capsules $50 for 5. Grams of yayo, kitty, MDMA $100. Eight balls $300 Coca tea bags $35 for 5. LSD $15/ hit. Crystal and Mexican Black $80/ gram. DMT vape $120. Lean bottles $2,000.*

I have no idea what a lean bottle is. So I text him back, *Just a gram of yayo, brotha. Thanks!*

I lie back on my bed and close my eyes. More "Stuntarinos" texts are coming in, but I've silenced them. After a few minutes, I text Raj again.

I'm in the Convention Center District.

He sends me the address of a parking lot outside of town in Jefferson Parish. Some emergency veterinary clinic that's sure to be closed at midnight. I put my clothes back on.

My black minivan is invisible in the vet clinic parking lot. No sounds but frogs and rustling trees. After ten minutes, a lanky, ghost-like Latino boy appears in the darkness. He climbs into my van. "Hey, slug," he says, and we bump fists. Then he puts his phone face down on the center console and dumps cocaine all over it. "This stuff will freeze your nose off it's so good. Here, try some."

I do a line, and he does one, and we agree that it's good.

"You want an eight ball, or a gram?"

BARBARIC FURY

HALONA TEXTS ME.

You're going to need a physical therapist while you're there. Can I come visit you?

We're downstairs at the Wollcroft Hotel at 7 a.m. Four people from the stunt team are here. They're obvious because of their biceps, baseball caps, and the word STUNTS on all their T-shirts, hats, and duffel bags. At least they don't say something embarrassing like "NAMASTE IN BED." They've already been to the gym. I recognize one of them from social media. The other three are strangers.

"What's up," I say, pulling up to a stop near them, resting an elbow on the wall, hair down, beard wild, sunglasses on. "I'm Lex."

At once they animate, stand up and shout, "What's up!" All four of them give me a one-armed hug-handshake as if I'm receiving an award. A tall, very white, man-child-looking guy says, "Lex played all the robots in the last *Terminator* movie." And the rest of them say, "Dope," and "Loved that movie."

"What's your name?" I ask him.

"I'm Target, bro," he says. "That there's Pit Mix, Sadie, and Leon."

My chest relaxes, and the room brightens a little, as I inhale, tasting the smells of hotel disinfectants and continental breakfast. Far away rain. Now I'm my real self again. These stuntmen respect me. I hadn't even considered that. At what point did I stop respecting myself? Hibernating in my room for a day and a half with nothing but cocaine and booze and audiobooks? It felt like my path at the time. I thought I was following my heart. But this is much better! This is more *me*.

Three of the stunt performers ride together. Target, Sadie, and Pit Mix, in Target's minivan. I'll introduce you to them all later. But for now, just know that Sadie is kind of hot. She's older, probably forty or close thereabout, and of course she's muscular, a little tarnished. The other two men are grunts. I look forward to getting to know them. I've heard stories about Target. Great ones. He's the guy who jumped off the roof into a dumpster, but they put the wrong dumpster there and instead of landing on a bunch of pads, he crashed into a mountain of garbage. He climbed out of the dumpster unharmed, without so much as a scratch on him. That's the stuff of legends right there.

Target, Sadie, and Pit Mix tell me they're going to the Ochsner Gym before rehearsal to get a membership, because the hotel gym sucks.

Leon rides with me. He's young and loose and janky, with an energy that says, "weed gummies." He wiggles a lot, and squints at the world through amused, lonely eyes. My minivan is waiting in a parking structure across the street from The Wollcroft. Leon and I gab at each other as we cross the street, then toss our bags into the back of the van. It turns out Leon is Ben Schilling's stunt double, so we'll be seeing a lot of each other in the next few months. We're both focused on becoming friends, talking optimistically, not looking at the minivan's center console, as I pull out of the dim parking structure, emerging into the bright sunlight of Calliope Street, and merging onto the highway.

Halona texts me. *So? Am I coming to visit you?*

I laugh, nervously. "Hey, Leon. This girl I met at a bar wants to come visit me—"

"Dude!" he interrupts.

"I know!" I say. "I mean, she'd be fun and all. But I really want to focus on the work, you know?"

"No," he says, *"dude!"* He's looking down at the center console, drawing my attention to it. Cocaine is scattered everywhere, from when Raj and I had divvied it the night before. My heart strikes a dissonant power chord.

"Oh, shit!" My face goes red hot. I want to rip it off. "Looks like someone broke into the van!" I swipe the coke all over the place. Some of it lands on Leon's pants. I push down on a good-looking rock with my fingertip and rub it all over my teeth and gums. "His loss," I say, swerving out of my lane for a second. "These roads are fucked. How does anybody drive here?"

Leon laughs. "Don't worry about that." He waves his hand toward the floor of the van. "We're the Schilling guys, now. God knows what *his* center console looks like."

I'm visualizing hearing aids and Viagra, but I take his meaning. I like this kid.

"But good luck getting this van into Mexico!" he says.

"My cat would love this van," I say back.

We're able to grab some breakfast at a District Donuts near the stages. The cashier looks like she's sixteen, triple-D breasts, and at once I'm feeling better about things. Leon doesn't seem to notice her, but he just about loses it when he tastes the pork belly taco. "These eggs are like fucking crazy!" he says. "And this is the biggest piece of pork belly I've ever seen!"

So here we are, making movies as well as friends. Eating the biggest pieces of pork belly we've ever seen, and eggs that are like fucking crazy, chatting away like skeletons in a graveyard. Everything has a carte blanche feeling, which identifies that jittery look of hopefulness Ed Fury wore in that first Zoom meeting. Things are going well.

We find the entrance to Nimh Studios off a pothole-riddled service road in the ironworks district. The road is unmarked. Driving in, there's a small security booth with a black woman in it vetting credentials. "Hello!" I say. "We're here with *Everyone's Frankenstein*. Stunt department." I jerk a thumb at Leon.

She directs us to a large gravel parking lot, straight to the back. From there, it's anyone's guess where our stage is.

Leon and I drag our stunt bags down the pebbly hill toward the compound, and the few people we see are black men with large baseball caps smoking cigarettes. Transpo, obviously. They wouldn't know where the stunt rehearsal is. But I'm reminded that distinguishing vagrants to their departments is something useful that I've learned to trust. Early in my career, I had been discouraged and often bewildered that no one wears a name tag or a damned department label. They're just a bunch of people doing stuff. Best to get out of their way. But over time, I've sharpened it down. The wide-brimmed baseball caps and cigarettes are transpo. The tanned, wily-eyed crackheads are construction. Women covered in tattoos are either makeup or wardrobe, unless they're under twenty-four, in which case they might be a PA. The dull, neatly put together people are actors. Smoking hot bombshells are the celebrity's assistants, or actors. Young to middle age Jewish people are writers. If they look like office workers, then they probably work in an office.

The director could be any walk of life. Young, old, transgender, mixed race—you'll never know. But I saw David Morley in that first Zoom meeting, so I don't need to worry about that. All I have to do is keep my smart-Alec mouth (or in my case, smart-*Alex* mouth) agreeably shut, until all the directors, stunt coordinators, and producers are out of the room, at which point my first smart-Alex remark will be something like, "Hey, in *Everyone's Frankenstein,* is 'everyone's' possessive, or is it a compound of 'everyone is?'" The latter makes more sense to me, as I understand the message in Mary Shelley's original text. Frankenstein's monster feels unlovable, dejected, lonely and hideous. Just like everyone.

Everyone's Frankenstein, sometimes.

At the bottom of the gravel path, Leon and I come to three sound stages, each with loading docks that face one another in an enormous U-shape, square patch of parking lot between them.

I look around for some stunt-looking people.

"Where the hell are we going?" I say to Leon. "There's no sign, and it's not on the call sheet."

"Stage C, bro," he says. "It's in the group text."

"Oh," I say. "Of course." And then I recognize with horror where I am.

I was here two days ago for my wardrobe fitting. The costume shop is attached to Stage C, the stunt gym. Remember that, dummy? No, you don't. Because that particular extension of your mind hotel was demolished by a big white, nose-numbing wrecking ball, and now you have to rebuild.

I clock the steel door in the corner of Stage C and lead Leon to it. Placing my foot on the horizontal push bar, I kick it open, not too hard, but I act like it's hard, and I scream, "Hey, donkey fuckers!"

Everything is quiet and dim compared to the glare of outside, and my sunglasses darken everything further. Slowly, what comes into focus is four men, three of whom are crouched over their work. The fourth is a tall, buff dude standing in the center of the room with his hands on his hips. They're all looking at us. Well, looking at me, more likely.

The riggers.

None of the stunt performers have arrived yet because I'm always thirty minutes early. The riggers are doing their preparations amid stacks of flight cases and toolboxes, dry-erase boards propped against winches with math equations scribbled across them. Genie lifts are parked at some angles. A small Italian-looking man has span sets slung over his shoulders. None of them seem humorous, but I know they're going to laugh at me later.

Fucked up my entrance.

I decide to keep it going, knowing nothing about rigging or what they do, aside from the very basics: stroke length, psi, pendulum physics, decelerations, sandbags, heavy drinking after work. The riggers also manage the crash pads: eight-inchers, four-inchers, panel mats, scenic pads, tombstones, and giant Port-a-Pits.

"What's up, guys," I say.

"What's up, guys," Leon says, like an echo.

I'm walking around the giant space, taking it all in while Leon warms up his body. Eventually Target comes through the steel door, talking about how "this guy's head was *all* the way off!" Sadie and Pit Mix take up the rear. All three of them are on One-Wheels.

Pit Mix says, "These are videos of people killing themselves?"

"Well," Target explains, "they're like fail videos."

"But people die in them?"

"I mean, it doesn't *say* they die, but . . . yeah, maybe. Come on. They're doing stupid shit."

The first day of stunts goes well. A lot of filling out paperwork and hauling truckloads of cardboard boxes for box catchers into the space. We're unloading mats. We're watching previz videos and camera tests. I'll explain box catchers and previz videos a bit later on.

We all drive to a location downtown. It's an historic building, an old American National Bank. It's abandoned now, and a prime location to build a theater in. We look at the balconies and talk about how safe it is to jump off them.

We fold together a few hundred cardboard boxes, work an hour past lunch, and then call it a day.

I have to ride back to the stages from the bank location to get my minivan. When I get there, I sneak into the kitchen for some good snacks to take home. I'm hoping for Cheez-Its, Wolfblood's favorite.

Near the kitchen are some offices. Patricia, the producer is in her office. She's watching a video, wearing a mask like everyone else. Her hands are resting lightly on her knees, head slightly tilted as she studies the screen, unmoving.

"Hi Patricia," I say. "I'm Lex." As I take a step inside the office, I see the video she's watching is a previz from earlier rehearsals in pre-pre-production.

Patricia turns slowly around to look at me. Her eyes appear haunted. I shift on my feet a little and look down at my hands. "Lex," she says. "How's everything going with rehearsals?"

"Well, it's the first day," I say. "Lotta moving gear around and like, paperwork. The location looks amazing, though."

"Which one?"

"The bank."

The eyes above her mask are dead. "Oh yes," she says. "Frankenstein's lair. That's a historic building."

"I know," I say. "I can't wait to destroy it."

"Me too."

"Lex!" Ed Fury is thundering toward me down the hallway, his hands curled into fists. "What are you doing back here?"

"I'm meeting Patricia," I say. "She's cool."

His face goes purple. "Come with me," he says. Fury and I walk silently, ten steps to where we're still in earshot of Patricia. It occurs to me that the posters on the wall, old-timey movie bills featuring Clarke Gable and Clint Eastwood are somehow sinister. Not in any real way, only in the context of this hallway.

"What the hell are you doing?" Fury says. His eyes are bloodshot, and fluttering. *It's the first day,* I think. *Holy shit.*

"I was walking down the hall, and I saw Patricia," I say. "I wanted to meet her."

"Why are you back here?"

"Because I had to get a key fob from production. And grab my new script. It was left in your office." Fury is still annoyed, so I say more. "I just saw Patricia and wanted to meet the woman I've been texting with. She's the one who hired me—and you, you hired me too. And I just thought . . ."

"No, dude," he says.

I look down in shame. Fury's tight pants are bulging in the thighs, so I return my gaze to his fraying face.

"If Patricia wants to meet with you," he says, "I'll let you know."

"Well, OK."

Pause.

"I'll see you tomorrow, Lex." Fury stares down the length of the hallway, waiting for me to leave.

My nostrils flare once. "OK," I say. "See you later."

I don't sleep well because I end up looking at the swimming pool. Hours are lost, trapped inside my window. Later I have restless legs, and my knees are jerking everywhere. It happens when I don't smoke weed. At some point in the night, I startle awake, sure that I felt an earthquake. I look at the Christmas lights hanging across the bed. Not moving.

Louisiana doesn't get a lot of earthquakes—not big ones, anyways. I looked it up. But it is understood that a large seismic event cannot be ruled out, as geological changes are often unpredictable, especially with the increased amount of oil drilling which surrounds New Orleans.

Earthquakes are my only irrational fear. People always say, "That's not an irrational fear, you were *in* an earthquake! You have every right to be afraid." But I say no. I understand the sentiment, of course; both of my dogs were killed in the Northridge Quake, and my face was gashed up by dance trophies and glass. But that's no reason for me cower every time an unexpected jolt happens, thirty years later.

After texting Halona a dozen times, I realize she might be crazy. She sends me a photo of a litter of kittens, with a text message that says, "They're going to die if no one adopts them."

So, I sleep maybe two hours.

Two very thirsty hours.

THE STUNTED MAN

WALL SCORPION

SECOND DAY, AND I'm shuddering down the gravel path from the parking lot with Leon toward the stages. It's 7:30 a.m. and hot already. Sweat rolls down my face like snowmelt.

Aurora texts me, and I read it while walking, gravel crunching underfoot.

Wolfblood killed a rat, she writes. *She's not feeling well.*

Cold flashes through my body. This is a false start. The second day is supposed to be Victory Day, but now I'm all storm clouds and trepidations. I gently open the small steel door and enter the quiet, cavernous sound stage.

Nobody's here yet, so I immediately set to work on making room in the little trash can next to the folding table that hasn't been emptied, squashing empty smoothie cups and old Covid masks down so I can throw something away. After five minutes I yell, "Dammit!"

Leon stops putting on his boxing gloves and looks at me. "Lex, you good over there?"

I grumble and put my hands on my hips. I've taken out two trash bags, but now there's no bag to put in the bin. "I need some bags, man."

The door clangs open, and Target, Sadie, and Pit Mix appear on their One-Wheels, accompanied by the end of another conversation. Target is waving his hands in the air. "Thirteen stair falls!" he says. "Nine hundred dollars!"

"Fuck that shit," Pit Mix says, swirling his One-Wheel to a stop. His round belly and blue sniper eyes distinguish him as our lead driver.

It's a conversation about stunt adjustments. They're always talking shop. Target arrives at his point. "That dude *sucks* at A.D.J.'s. Never work for Connor Glick."

"Oh, I know," Sadie says. "He's the worst."

"Fury is actually good with stunt adjustments," Target says. Then he looks at me. "What's up, Lex!"

"Yeah," I say. "As long as you don't put your hand down or try to save yourself from being decapitated by a dinner plate."

Horrible silence. Everyone's looking at me.

Eventually Target says, "Um, Fury's just trying to look good, you know? He doesn't want you fidgeting around when the producers and director are there. He's thinking about the big picture, you know? The *film*. That's a good thing." Target leans his One-Wheel against the folding table.

"But take it with a grain of salt, Lex. Always protect yourself. It's only money." He looks at the trashcan next to his One-Wheel, grimaces, and places his empty smoothie cup on the table. "Anyways," he says, "your safety ain't worth Fury's reputation. That's like, nothing to you." Target jumps up and down a few times, then runs onto the floor and throws a front flip. "Woooo!" he shouts. "You're Lex Mercier, dude! You're a fucking legend!"

I turn my back to him, pretend to dig around in my stunt bag. "Ed *Fury*," I pout, putting my sunglasses back on. "More like Ed . . . ummm . . ."

Sadie continues. "He's really good at what he does."

"Damn straight," Target says. "He's gonna be a director someday."

Leon is shadow boxing in the corner, wearing a Puma track suit and headphones, and I'm still thinking, *Blurry? Furry? Unsure-y?*

Target says, "He's directing second unit on this one. It's gonna be dope."

"Have you read the script?" I ask, not turning around.

"No," Target says, throwing jabs and doing twists with his waist, jumping up and down some more.

"It's good," I say. "This movie's gonna be awesome."

"Fuck yeah!" he agrees.

Sadie says, "I ain't making no Amazon Prime shit."

"Same here!" Leon calls from across the giant room, punching the air.

"Well," I say pessimistically, "David Morley's last two films were Amazon Prime movies. But this one's gonna be different. Universal and shit. Big release. Fury's got everything on the line."

"He's gonna crush it though," Target says. He's kicking his legs as high as he can, then jumping up and down again.

Leon calls out, "Yeah, he got this shit!" and throws a side flip.

I take my sunglasses off and head onto the floor, ready to start loosening up. "I'm sure he does," I say. "Otherwise, we'll have to start calling him Ed *Failure-y.*"

They all look at me.

Luisa, another stunt performer, appears in the doorway with her dog, a shepherd mix with white shaggy fur.

"Who's the . . . *what?*" I shout and run slowly over to the dog. "Who's this?"

"That's Shredder," Luisa says.

"Shredder! That's a great name! Look at her eyes!"

"He's a boy."

"He's a boy!" The dog sprouts a dick in a millisecond of my imagination. "I love him. Good boy, yes!"

Luisa looks pleased. "Is Fury here yet?"

"Haven't seen him," I say.

"Fury's in the office. He'll be here soon." Jin Hoon, the assistant stunt coordinator, is assembling rubber rifles next to the folding table. When did Jin get here? Did he hear what I just said? I'm going to assume not, since I haven't been murdered yet. Schoolyard names are certainly grounds for murder in the stunt biz.

Cripple's here too. Is there another door somewhere?

"What's up, Jin," I say. He looks at his phone and doesn't answer me.

A wardrobe girl walks along the far wall of the stunt gym, disappears through the costume shop door in the corner. I haven't seen her before.

Jin Hoon retires his phone to his back pocket and says, "Fury will be here in five minutes. When he arrives, we're gonna talk through all the action sequences."

Everyone says, "Dope!" and, "Yes sir!"

It's 8:10 a.m., and I'm feeling pretty warm, so I go into the bathroom to vape a bunch of nicotine and text Aurora.

How's Bloody doing? Is she OK?

I get no reply.

"It starts with Pit Mix and Lex coming around the corner," Fury says. "They're stalkers, wearing all black. They sneak up behind Frankenstein, and the three of them have an eight-beat combo." Fury is pacing back and forth by the folding table. The Stuntarinos all face him like an audience of bloodhounds.

He's talking about Frankenstein's monster, but I'm not going to correct him. Anyways Dr. Frankenstein is basically The Creature's father, right?

Fury continues. "Frankenstein push-kicks Lex in the chest, BAM! knocking him into Pit Mix, and they stumble backwards. Then Frankenstein takes a wooden post and swings it at both of them. Pit Mix does a big reaction, and Lex does a big fucking Wall Scorpion into the side of the cottage, and smashes his fucking head, BAM! At this point, the villagers are coming for the farmer and Frankenstein. They're all screaming, torches and pitchforks, that kind of thing. Sadie and Cripple come over the hill and get hit by a flying wheelbarrow."

Sadie raises her hand and asks, "What's a flying wheelbarrow?"

Fury grins. "It's just a regular wheelbarrow," he says. "At this point in the scene, Frankenstein is ripping the support pylons off the cottage's balcony and flinging wheelbarrows at the townspeople. He's also gonna fling other things, like a horse trough, let's see, a haystack, and a wagon."

"How's he gonna fling a haystack with a wooden post?" I blurt.

Fury looks at me. "Anyways," he says, "Sadie and Cripple get hit by the wheelbarrow and go down. BAM!" He punches the palm of his left hand, hard. "Then the farmer and his wife come out onto the cottage's balcony to look around. They see the townspeople approaching, but they can't see Frankenstein underneath the balcony. Frankenstein *spears* the pylon through the floor of the balcony. He *misses* the farmer and his wife, but then tears the whole thing down and they both die in a crumbly mess. That's gonna be Luisa and Target."

"Fuck yeah," Target says.

"That's when we get to the real fighting." Fury starts to pace around the room, past the row of rubber rifles and onto the mat, navigating the foam rollers and massage guns that litter the floor. Stuntarinos follow him with their faces. "We have a couple of dead mans and a huge ratchet pull that I'm calling the 'home run.' Whoever wants it. At one point we're gonna have the monster go back into the cottage and come out dragging a stove with wood burning in it. He's gonna throw the stove at fucking Jin and Cripple and they'll do a big reaction, and a partial fire burn."

Cripple isn't listening. He's sitting at the folding table, apart from the group, editing something on his laptop. Large, spherical shoulders arch out from his tight-fade haircut. Cripple's concentrated expression is wearing glasses, looking very sexy-nerd.

"Then the climax happens," Fury continues. "The town's *oil man* has constructed a rolling wagon with an oil tank on top of it with a hose. They're gonna spray the cottage down and burn the fucking shit out of it. The townspeople hate the farmer as much as the monster because the farmer basically raised him, taught him to speak and like, hunt and stuff. Frankenstein goes back into the house to find more cool shit to fight with, and he doesn't see the oil man spraying the side of the cabin. The townspeople throw some torches and *BOOM!* House goes up. We think Frankenstein's dead, even though it's still the beginning of the movie, and of course here comes the epic shot: Frankenstein emerging out of the flames in fucking gorgeous silhouette, dragging behind him the burning corpse of the farmer. He has a moment—that's you, Leon—and then he chucks the farmer at the oil tank. *BOOOM!* Lots of fire burns."

Everyone cheers.

"We'll have a dummy for the farmer."

"Dammit!" Target says.

"I know," Fury opens an energy drink and chugs it. "I told Morley we could do it, but he really wants to see it fly through the air. And it's too expensive."

"Alright."

"So that's the cottage fight. Pretty simple! We'll grab some ND guys for the easy gags, and you guys will dial in the cool shit."

Everyone applauds and shouts stuff like, "Fuck yeah," and "let's fucking go!"

I'm a little concerned about that first part. Wall Scorpion? I haven't done one of those in years. I used to be famous for them, but ever since I fractured my neck in Hawaii, I've sort of toned it down. This, however—here and now—is not the place for toning it down.

A regular Scorpion is when you dive-bomb the ground onto your face, so your legs flip over your head like a scorpion's tail. A Wall Scorpion (something I invented) is exactly the same thing, only against a wall or a tree. It's a beautiful two-beat action, the first of which is impaling your face into the wall, and the second is collapsing to the ground like a bag of bones. I've booked a lot of gigs with that move, but since Hawaii I've sort of willed that skill from people's memory. Younger people are doing it these days. Let them eat cake.

While the team is still chattering, I text Aurora again, quickly.

How's Bloody doing?

"Okay!" Fury shouts. Everyone falls silent. "Next, we have the hospital fight. This one is fucking epic! Everyone is gonna burn, and everyone is getting squibbed to fucking hell. Frankenstein has a huge fire burn. Leon, you're gonna have your hands full on this one."

"Dope," Leon says. "Fuck me up, boss."

Fury talks us through the hospital scene. It's a great piece. Lots of long takes, stair falls, operatic choreography. I'm doing another Wall Scorpion. This time on fire.

There are four large action sequences in *Everyone's Frankenstein*. The cottage fight, the hospital fight, the swamp fight, and the finale, in Frankenstein's lair.

The story takes place over a hundred-year span, so we'll be going from cottages and wagons to machine guns, hence the "everyone is getting squibbed to fucking hell" section.

They're going to make me shave my beard. I just know it. The swamp fight is all creatures, so we'll be wearing major prosthetics. And for that fire burn . . . I'll want to at least trim it.

She's not good, Aurora writes. *She's been lying on her side all day. Not curled up or anything.* She sends me a photo.

Wolfblood looks like roadkill. The stunt gym greys, and the place between my heart and stomach freezes.

Oh my god, please take her to the vet, right now if you can. I'll reimburse you whatever.

Leon shoulders up beside me. "What up, bitch," he says. "You got plans for lunch?"

My arm is tired from holding up my phone, so I relax it and say, "No dude."

"We're all going to the Vietnamese place, Let's Pho."

"That's the name of the restaurant?"

"Yeah," he says. "Why? Does that mean something?"

I twist around to look at Leon, framing his face in tunnel vision. "Yeah," I say. "It means they hit bedrock digging at that pun."

Leon's mouth opens and closes. "Are you OK, bro?"

I'm not sure that I am.

"Yeah, I'm fine," I say. "My cat's sick. I'm feeling very far away."

"Oh, damn," he says. He puts a hand on my shoulder and stops shifting on his feet, somehow morphing into a grownup. "I'm sorry, dude."

My phone buzzes in my hand. *I have a client in ten minutes. I'm already at the studio. I can take her after that.*

Aurora teaches private dance lessons for small children.

Please cancel your client, I text. *Children are not as important as cats. If it's a bacterium it can spread like wildfire in her—*

"Lex!" Fury shouts, walking briskly toward me.

I start. "Hey, Fury, what's up?"

"We're going to have you meet with Ben Schilling after lunch," he says. He glances down at his Apple Watch. "You too, Leon."

"You got it, boss," Leon says.

"Yes sir," I say.

Fury sniffs and rubs his nose. "I can't be there because I have a meeting, but Jin will be there to supervise."

"Supervise?" I say.

"Yeah," he says. "Because I'll be in a meeting."

"Yeah, but . . . supervise who?"

"You, dude!"

I look toward Leon, then back at Fury. Fury's eyes are wide and twitchy. "OK," I say. "Let's supervise this shit."

Let's Pho is very good. I was hungrier than I'd expected. However, there is one problem. I've mostly avoided mentioning quarantine and Covid-19 throughout this book, but I believe this part needs to be deliberated.

Aside from a few zombie shows, and some vague press events, I've spent most of the last two years in solitude. Eventually I grew accustomed to the confinement, not realizing that my soul was tethering itself to a pole, and gradually winding itself shorter. That pole was security. But that pole was also sovereignty and ego. And as the tether grew shorter, my sense of self blossomed into something glorious, however insular, and domesticated, like a mind hotel closed to anyone without a room key or staff ID. I became the caretaker of an empty hotel, my only job to maintain the boiler tank, making sure it doesn't overheat and explode.

Now I'm out—*way out*—in public, seated at a small table with six husky, wide-kneed stuntmen. My sense of self is overheating, steam hissing through the seams and screw holes of said boiler tank. I'm parked at the end of the table between Ed Fury and Leon, waiting desperately, doomstruck for my meal. Leon's knees are wiggling so much I want to punch them and leave. Then I can drive back to the stages and eat Slim Jim's and fruit snacks from the kitchen—fuck it.

But soon my food comes. Pork belly on white rice with a cracked egg, and before long I'm an optimist again.

Ben Schilling strides into the stunt gym with giant steps, leather pants and two sugar-free Red Bulls in one hand, a script in the other. His assistant walks behind him. Schilling takes in the space, recognizes it perhaps, then puts his stuff down on the folding table. He seems like he needs directions, or his vision isn't very good.

Jin says, "Mr. Schilling! Hello!"

Jin, Leon, and I form a small greeting triangle.

He walks over to us. "Ben Schilling," he says. "Prayers and greetings." He slaps his thighs and bows tightly.

I take a massive gulp from my coffee cup, burp a little and say, "What's up, I'm Lex." He raises his eyebrows at me, showing all the bags surrounding his unmistakable eyes.

We don't warm up, and we don't go onto the floor. The first day is just chatting. No stress. Jin is saying some things that are poignant and neutral, and I'm smiling to mask my contempt, allowing it. Then he segues into movement talk.

"So," Jin says, "when you're fighting, you want to stay loose, you know? You want to keep your body moving." He starts shifting forward and back. "Like a cobra!" he says. "When a cobra wants to strike, it *glides* a little. Or a boxer, always moving."

Ben Schilling watches Jin. Then he shakes his head disapprovingly.

"No," he says. "That's not it. That's not how I would do it."

Jin stops moving. "OK. So how would you do it?"

Schilling is silent. Eventually, he sees something on the floor that gives him an idea. "Well," he says, "I would be completely still. Then, I would float up into the air . . . And then I'd come down and eat his head! That's what I would do."

"OK," Jin says. "Great. So how would you do that? Like with your body?"

Ben Schilling puts his hands on his hips and leans back. "Well, I don't know," he says.

"Hey, let's slow this down a little," I interject, throwing Jin a wink. "I don't think Frankenstein can float in the air, anyways."

"He can't do that?" Schilling says.

"No," I say. "Just a lot of walking and crawling and fighting."

"Well," Jin says, "if you're going to be tackled or leaping through the air, we'll probably have Leon doing it."

Schilling looks to Leon and says, "How are you?" He does his tight bow again and adds, "Of course. I'm not doing *that.*"

Jin chuckles agreeably and says, "We can put you on a wire though, if you want. Somewhere."

Schilling thinks for a moment and then nods. "Yeah. OK."

Back in the hotel room, I need comfort food, bad. So, I fry up some burgers with American cheese and lots of mayo and pickles. It's very good. I sit on the bed and look at the swimming pool. It's full of dark water, empty of people. I try my best to dream, my eyes on the dark rectangle, my mind on the cocaine that's wrapped up in the Excedrin bottle in the bathroom. This isn't forever. Earlier today, I dumped out the few remaining beers I had left, because they had been talking to me all night, making it hard to sleep. Turns out I can still hear them anyways.

I listen to the *We Sold Our Souls* audiobook for two hours while staring into the pool.

Eventually, I take some CBD and a Melatonin, and as visions of a desperate Wolfblood drift over me, I fall asleep.

BOX CATCHER

THE THIRD DAY Target shows up with a smashed rental car, Sadie and Pit Mix in tow, trying not to look morose. I'm out front by the dumpsters smoking a cigarette as they drive by, and I'm still there as they One-Wheel down the gravel hill to the stages.

"Morning, guys," I say. "What was that?"

"Target crashed his rental car," Sadie replies.

"Well, what happened?"

I open the metal door to stage C, and as we shuffle inside Target yells, "Goddam truck stopped on the fucking highway!"

"But they do that all the time," I say. Then a thought occurs to me. "Wait, you hit a truck? And survived?"

"It was a pickup," he clarifies.

From a clumsy downward dog position, Pit Mix chimes in: "If it's a rental, don't be gentle!" which alarms me of something horrifying, having to do with prostitutes.

Target counters Pit Mix by saying, "How about: if it's a rental, don't dismantle the antilock brake system without telling me."

"You don't need that ABS," Pit Mix says. "You were tailgating that guy."

Target is too insulted to respond. Instead, he turns his attention to me and says, "How's your cat doing, bro?"

I'm looking at the trash bin which hasn't been emptied. "Not great," I say. "I think she has a bacterial condition called 'botulism,' because she ate a poisoned rat."

"Oh, no!" he says. "Fucking New York, am I right?"

"Well, it's bad," I explain. "She's really sick. But what's worse is that sometimes these cases can lead to paralysis. She's on meds now, so hopefully it doesn't come to that. Anyways, she'll bounce back quickly." I couldn't appear less confident, and Target registers this.

"Dude, I'm sorry."

"I'm sorry, Lex," Pit Mix and Sadie both say, and I'm grateful for feeling terrible without having to hide it.

Leon is shadow boxing on the mat with his headphones in. I place my breakfast sandwich wrapper on top of the trash pile and head on to the floor to start warming up.

"So how did your first rehearsal with Ben Schilling go?" Sadie asks.

"Pretty good." I'm buttoning up a gray long-sleeve flannel. "Jin was there, although I'm not sure why."

"I heard he was supervising," she says.

I stop putting on my flannel. "Well, yeah," I say. "But I don't know if Schilling likes him very much. It felt more like I was supervising Jin."

After a moment, Sadie says, "I hear you, Lex. But hey, we're all supervising each other, you know? We're a team. We look out for each other."

"That's total bullshit," I say. "I'm not supervising Mike and the riggers."

Sadie picks up a rubber handgun and throws a shoulder roll, landing in a crouched low-ready position, perfectly grounded. "The riggers are different," she says. She blows a strand of red hair off her cheek. Then lowering her gun, she adds, "But yeah. That was total bullshit."

Fury, Jin, Cripple, and Luisa arrive at eight. Fury walks stiffly, as if he sat on a cactus. Jin is twirling a butterfly knife, open and closed, open and closed, looking at no one.

I call out, "Hey, Luisa, where's Shredder?"

"OK guys!" Fury shouts, placing his empty smoothie cup on the folding table. "Welcome to the first day of pre-viz!"

Everyone goes, "Woooo!"

A previz, or "pre-visualization" is a bone-crushing video sequence created by the stunt team. It's designed to inform the director and VFX guys exactly how the action of a scene will be realized. The more complicated the action sequence is, the more involved the previz, especially when it comes to rigging. The stunt performers film it piece by piece, which can take as long as two weeks to shoot, or as little as one day. Once the previz is completed and the director has signed off, it is used by the camera department, VFX, stunt doubles and the director to establish exactly how they will shoot the scene on the day. By then the stunt department will have perfected the rigging, dialed in the choreography, and made sure all the story beats are there.

Some stunt teams have bare bones previzes, shot on an iPhone, edited loosely. Other stunt teams try to invent an Oscar category, belaboring everything from lighting, editing and blood effects, to music and foley. Barbaric Fury is one of the latter, as I'm sure you've already guessed. They use expensive cameras, shoot everything twenty times, and edit throughout the nights.

A lot of box catchers are involved in previzes. Not only to show the falls, but as safety nets when action is happening on balconies or ledges. The boxes are also used to build mockup dimensions of the sets, like hallways and furniture. All of it is made from cardboard boxes.

Remember that gray flannel I just put on? I'll be wearing it for the next ten days. For continuity.

The first previz we aim to tackle is the final fight, in Frankenstein's lair. For this, we must use the actual bank location because the riggers need the space to build all the aerial stuff. There's a ton of wire work in this scene, and not a lot of space to design it in without first building a truss.

Fury had talked through the finale on the first day, but only vaguely. He knew he'd be talking and walking it in the space, so we're all pretty curious about who's doing what when we get to the old National American Bank building on Carondelet.

The dark building has been gutted and abandoned, but it still remains glorious in its magnitude. There's nothing in the main room except a wrap-around balcony, enormous marble columns, and a vaulted, pressed metal ceiling. Construction equipment has been clustered into two corners to make room for our rehearsal. Dust particles sparkle in the aquatic morning light.

The rigging truck is parked out front, loaded with crash mats and stacks of flattened cardboard boxes.

Wanderers on the street steal suspicious glances, as the stunt team unloads all the mats and fifteen hundred flattened cardboard boxes. Once that's done, the doors to Frankenstein's lair close, shutting us in, and Fury begins his walk n' talk.

"What's up, *guys,*" Fury says, grinning like a machine. He looks around at everyone, and I'll be damned if his smile doesn't drop a little when he sees me. Barely at all, but I notice it. "It's going to be a crazy couple of weeks," he says. "You're all gonna be on wires."

The gist of the scene is this: The FBI and a SWAT team infiltrate Frankenstein's lair. They fan out and take positions on the ground floor, but the main room is empty. As they ascend the stairwell to the second floor, Frankenstein bursts out from what we already know is his laboratory. By this point in the film, the "monster" has become the "scientist," and has invented his own special weapons—the most awesome of which is his lightning gun. He has also created eight new monsters as prototypes of what he hopes will one day be his wife. Alas, none of them are capable of love, and all of them are too hideous to wed, even for Frankenstein. But Frank can't destroy the monsters because of his big, magnanimous heart. Instead, he keeps them in a playroom as pets. The playroom sits at the end of the second-floor corridor, the door closed and always bolted.

So, the SWAT team charges up the stairs, assault rifles ready, and Frankenstein bursts out from his laboratory with his lightning gun and blazes them all into oblivion, kind of a *Scarface* moment. Through the smoke, a frag grenade sails past Frankenstein's head and rolls to the end of the balcony where it clatters and then explodes, destroying the door of the creatures' playroom.

Deformed female figures spill out through the doorway. They crawl onto the ledge of the balcony and drop onto the first floor like cockroaches. A large battle ensues. In the script it simply says: "All hell breaks loose, and everyone fucking mutilates each other." So, we have some artistic liberties there.

We'll hire a team of stuntwomen for the creatures. I'll recommend a few of my friends to Fury.

The first thing we set up to shoot is the eight monsters jumping off the balcony. You guessed it: box catcher. The next twenty minutes are spent building five hundred boxes and stacking them three-high under the balcony. We place enormous Port-a-Pits on top of the catcher so we can land on our feet. When that's done, all eight of us walk up the stairs, climb onto the ledge of the balcony and look down.

"Does it feel OK?" Fury shouts from the first floor.

"Yes sir!" we all agree. And since Cripple is on the ledge with us, Fury is holding the camera.

"Alright, let's shoot one!" he says. "We're gonna do the drop in two groups, so it looks random. Lex, Target, Jin, Luisa, and Leon, you're group one. Pit Mix, Cripple and Sadie, group two. Got it?"

"Copy!"

"I'm gonna yell, 'three, two, one, go!' The first group jumps on 'one.' The second group jumps on 'go.' Are we clear?"

"Yes sir!"

"Copy!"

"Stunts, set?"

"Set!"

Mike and the riggers are standing in the far corner of the room by some toolboxes and sawhorses, arms folded, looking bored.

"OK!" Fury shouts. "We are rolling! And . . . *three, two, one—*"

I leap off the balcony and drop onto the Port-a-Pit, landing in a crouched position. The Port-a-Pit that I land on is old and baggy. Because of this, the half of the Port-a-Pit I don't land on balloons out with air, and when Pit Mix hits it a second later, it launches me off the box catcher into the air like a teeter board.

Now, I used to be in the circus, but I'm not anymore. I flip into the air and crash down onto the floor, which is stone, or cement, or Masonite, I don't know. I *do* know that it's as hard as fucking Cannibal Corpse's fourth album, and my body is vibrating in a terrible way, flushed with heat. Immediately, my vision greys and my hearing mutes.

There's a commotion. A few people are laughing. Target's in stitches, and someone says, "That was nasty, bro!" with what sounds like approval.

Fury is grinning, but behind his face is total panic. "Lex, what the fuck was that?" He's leaning over me, looking deep into my eyes, checking for a concussion.

"I'm OK," I say. Then, because my inhibiters are scattered, I add, "Thanks for asking."

I hold out my hand. He yanks me to standing and says, "Why did you do that?"

"I was launched! Look, I need two minutes."

"You good for another one?"

"Yeah. Two minutes."

I walk as casually as I can across the room to my stunt bag, while Pit Mix explains to everyone what happened. The riggers are there, and they're worried. Mike gives me another concussion check.

"Are you OK?" Mike says. "That was fucking gnarly."

"It hurt like a bitch," is my reply.

"But are you OK? That looked totally crazy."

"I'm fine," I say. "Rung my bell. Just need thirty seconds."

I know they don't believe me. Experienced riggers can sense apprehension from a mile away.

I eat four Tylenol and three Advil, washing them down with a gulp of CBD oil. The riggers see this, but they don't wince. My stomach immediately starts burning.

I pull out my phone to look at a picture of Wolfblood, something to comfort me. I have a new text from Aurora, but I don't open it because I'm too close to crying, and I might not be able to handle what she has to say. Instead, I look back at Mike and say, "Your Port-a-Pit is donkey-fucked." The compassion in his face almost crumbles me, so I turn and walk slowly back to the stairwell, rejoining the others on the second floor, returning to one.

I consider throwing a four-incher on top of the Port-a-Pit to soften my impending launch, but I decide it might get in the way of Pit Mix's landing, and I don't want to risk him rolling an ankle, so I leave the setup as it is. Peering down at the box catcher from the second-floor precipice, I hear Fury shout, "Lex, you need to jump higher this time! That last jump was fucking lame!"

"Copy that!" I shout back.

"We are rolling! Stunts, set?"

"Set!"

I get back to the hotel and pull some food out of the fridge. But once I have all the ingredients laid out, chicken thighs, onions, yogurt, and curry paste, I decide I'm not hungry. I put all the groceries back in the fridge and take a sparkling iced tea instead, then move toward the edge of the bed and look out the window into the courtyard. It's the same amount of nothing out there. *The city's popping,* I think. My guts are supplicating for action. Maybe the Wollcroft will get livelier on the weekends. To be honest, the only direction it could go from here would be a livelier one. But for now, it's just the dark swimming pool, and occasional guests heading either out or in.

I still don't feel like watching TV. A Ben Schilling movie sounds great now that I know the guy, but the thought of all that light and noise is even less appetizing than half-assed chicken thighs.

So, I put my headphones in and listen to Tragedy's second album. It's a fearsome one, guitar slides and thundering patterns. Soon I'm lost in the weight of it all, the feedback, the swarm of sound, and eventually I'm feeling better. There's a moment when I think I'm having heart palpitations. But really, I'm just hearing the music right.

The album ends, so I put on Tragedy's first album, because they're the angriest band I've ever heard, even with that bottle of Excedrin in the bathroom with the cocaine inside it singing "Happy Birthday, Mr. President" louder than everything.

After a few songs, my ears get tired, but my mind is still awake. I examine the dirty clothes scattered on the floor between the bed and the window.

Eventually, I lie down and jack off, but that only takes ten minutes, and my orgasm is weak. So, I look out the window some more. I text with Halona until she goes to sleep.

By now it's too late for Melatonin, and way too late for Advil PM. So I fold myself into bed and wait. I put on the *We Sold Our Souls* audiobook. It's good, but I have to turn it off because of all the toxic feminism. The book is too dark, even for me. Now there's nothing left to do but lie here and listen to the inner voices.

After two hours of sleep, I'm awake again.

It's 5 a.m., so I head down to the gym for some low-impact training.

The gym is small and freezing. The hotel managed to fit five television screens on the walls. One is turned off, and the other four are playing CNN. A commercial for pharmaceuticals segues into *The Lead with Jake Tapper*, probably a re-roll since it's 5 a.m. There he is, with his grey façade and his petrified, pants-full-of-shit expression, signaling to us that if he were to move just one muscle in his body he'll be electrocuted. I know the feeling, and it doesn't comfort me at all. There's going to be a blackout today, and escalating unemployment rates, and more cops murdering people, and storms because of the heatwave, and I have no idea where the goddamn remote control is, so I exit the gym and head back to my room. Anyways, my back feels like cold garbage. And it's too early for breakfast.

At 6:30 I go back downstairs, after managing another half hour of sleep.

Jin Hoon and Ed Fury requested to meet with me before work, so I'm riding solo today.

My rental van is not where I left it. It's three spaces over, and across the aisle. A chill scuttles up my back, and my legs stop walking. For some reason I turn around, making sure I haven't been followed. It looks like I haven't. As I slowly get into the van, observing the subtle changes in the smell, I know it's been used. Or stolen. The seat isn't in the right position. The foot pedals are too close. I get out of the van and check it for damages. When it seems OK, I get back in, adjust the seat, and drive to work.

The parking lot at the stages is muddy and loose, stony with puddles. A spooky thin mist floats above the ground, drifting between trailers, through chain link fences, along loading dock walls.

As I approach the stunt office in the hallway, I stop, hearing Jin and Fury's voices through the door. I can't make out what they're saying, but I hear the word "unhappy," and then Jin says clearly, "I don't think he's even showering." I knock on the door and use my key to enter.

Two small trash cans are in the room, both of them overflowing.

"Bro," Fury says.

I look at him blankly.

His hands are in fists, holding up invisible grocery bags. "We have to talk to you."

"Yeah," I say. "What's up."

Fury looks like a nightmare in this light, a two hundred fifty-pound explosive. "I've been talking to Morley," he says. "He likes you. He wants to book you as the Dead Assassin."

"Really?" I say. "Sweet!"

"Yeah, but we don't know about that." He pauses. "How's your body, dude? Are you even up for it?"

"Of course," I say. "What do you mean?"

"Well, you seem tired. And like, unfit."

"It takes you two minutes to stand up, bro," Jin says. This is the first thing he's spoken to me since the last time I worked for him, in 2018.

"Nah," I say, pulling my hands out of my pockets. "I'm good to go. Maybe a little slow these days, but I'm still ready to shred."

They look doubtful. When it's clear that neither of them will respond, I continue. "Does he want me to read? Let's do this! By the way, Fury, you're crushing it so far—"

"Yeah," Fury says. "He wants you to read." His hands are still in fists. "You're not gonna make me look bad, bro." This time it's not a question.

"Of course not," I say. "I'm healthy now. I'm sober—" *why the fuck did I say sober,* "and my body feels good . . . I mean, my hips do this little . . . thing, when it rains, but that's all. I'm good to go! I'll be a great Dead Assassin."

I want to swipe that fucking smile off of Jin's face.

"Sober," Fury says, dubiously.

"Yeah," I say. "Sober."

Fury glances at Jin, then back at me. "Right."

"Look, is this what you guys called me in to talk about? I mean, I'm more than happy to show up early, but you could've told me this anytime during rehearsal. Or in a text. With the sides."

"No," Fury says. "We have something else we want to talk to you about."

"OK," I say. "What is it?"

Fury draws in a stuttered breath and closes his eyes. "There's cocaine all over your fucking rental car."

I take a step back, despite myself. "Whoa," I say, "I can explain."

"I don't want you to explain," he barks. "You're on the list, bro. You get one fucking warning, that's it." Fury unclenches his hands, finally. "I don't want to fire you, dude. It'll make me look bad. But if you fuck up again, you're out!"

I know for a fact that Fury's way of firing people involves a sack over the head, a fatal bludgeoning, and a swampy grave somewhere in St. Charles Parish. I mean, I don't actually know that for a fact, but I definitely don't want to be the fact-checker.

"Yes sir," I say. "But listen, I really am sober—"

"Stop talking!" he says. "Just do your job. And go to the fucking gym. Like a man." Fury takes another breath, then says, "And don't you dare fuck this up."

He forgot to say *for me. "Don't you dare fuck this up for me."*

There is a silver lining here, believe it or not. I've finally figured out what Ed Fury rhymes with. It's a stretch, and a paint-by-numbers rhyme purist like my brother would definitely not accept it. But it works for me. Ed Fury, it turns out, kind of rhymes with "add insult to injury."

But hey, the Dead Assassin! That's cool. That's a big role. I mean it's a tiny role, but it's big for me. I'm gonna have my own booth at Comic Con forever. I'm gonna get laid at Comic Con forever! Things are looking up for me. God likes it when I'm sober. He's rewarding me.

I snatch a cup of coffee and a pickle from the crafty kitchen and walk noncommittally toward the stunt gym, thinking, *the Dead Assassin. Everyone in the world must wish that was their nickname in high school.*

I still have to audition though. I've read the script already, so I know the gist of his dialogue. There isn't much of it, which is good. This might actually work out. And Morley might let me keep my beard! I'm gonna be the *Bearded* Dead Assassin! That's why he wants me, right? Oh, how I wish I could've seen Fury's face when Morley brought it up. "How about Lex?" he would've said. And Fury would've eagerly agreed, all but falling to his knees. "*Absolutely,* sir! Lex is my best guy! I'll ask him right now!" The grinning, pandering, distrusting, deadlifting, body dysmorphic, misanthropic—

"Watch your face!" someone yells, and I flinch, throwing up my hands.

"Sorry. We're aging the costumes."

When I lower my hands, I see a girl. She's beautiful, especially in contrast to the stunt gym, which is gray and dark, even with the fluorescents on.

"You dropped your pickle," she says.

I'm stunned, because what I'm looking at is a medium height, young projection of my future. She's coated with bright, atomic-colored tattoos, and has pink and brown hair and white overalls with a notebook poking out of the front pocket. She's a rainbow on a goddamn waterfall.

"Hi," I say.

"Hi," she replies. "I'm Zelda. I'm with wardrobe."

"She's spraying shit on the costumes in here!" Target yells from the floor. Why is he here so early? Cripple's here too, setting up his computer gear and getting ready to edit before rehearsal starts.

I turn back to the girl, and once again I'm gob-smacked by her hectic beauty. I clear my throat. "Why are you spraying that shit on the costumes in here?"

"I'm just by the door," she says. "There's no air circulation in the costume shop, and we can't open the loading docks because of the heat."

"There's a blackout coming," I say.

"That's what they're saying, yeah. I'm just using your air conditioning if that's OK. And your door, for the draft." She gestures to her left with a large spray-pump bottle at the open steel door I just walked through.

My whiskers twitch. "You shouldn't spray that stuff in here. We're being physically active. And it smells really bad. There are cameras and computers in here that are sensitive. Please finish your work outside."

"But it's so hot out there," she says.

"Hey!" I look her dead in the face. "There are people risking their *lives* in here. Just do it. Please." I help her drag her wardrobe and gear outside. "I'm Lex, by the way."

She nods.

I pick up my pickle, bring it into the stunt gym, and place it on top of the trash pile.

CUDDLES WITH THE DYING

I NOW HASTEN to the more moving part of my story.

We continue working on previzes throughout the next three weeks, completing two large and complicated action sequences: the finale in Frankenstein's lair, and the hospital fight—the one with the flaming Wall Scorpion.

After the first few days, however, I start to get sick. I'm suffering chills and fevers, dizzy spells, and sometimes muffled spasms in front of everybody. I'm pointing at things that nobody sees, and I'm always sweating. At one point during a lunch break, Sadie has to convince me that there aren't any snakes in the bathroom.

So I decide, reluctantly, to reintroduce drugs into my system. *Responsibly* this time, not recklessly. And not without that withering sense of shame and resignation we all know too well. Once a compromise is established, we take a half a Xanax at night, and another half during the day, and that seems to help. No weed. No micro-dosing muscle relaxers for my teeth grinding. No peppery, nostalgic Jack Daniels, and no fentanyl because I'm out.

I don't touch any alcohol. If I were to drink as little as one beer, everyone would know.

By degrees, I start sleeping better, and I have wild, vivid dreams. The first two weeks are the usual nightmares—performing on stage unrehearsed, gunshot reports next to my head, Wolfblood lying on the ground skinned and bloody but still alive—normal stuff. But soon enough, the nightmares become kinder, and eventually I start looking forward to them.

After my dreams get better and my shakes go away, I fuck Zelda, the wardrobe chick, twice.

I book the Dead Assassin, so now I have to try on some flashy leather capes and costumes. Zelda and I seem to be hitting it off. One time we hit it off in a changing room while she whispered sweet confessions into my slobbery ear. Some women move fast, emotionally.

I, on the other hand, am running on four flats.

I have a few prosthetic tests for my face and hands. They're so horrifying I can't even look at myself. The swamp scene is going to be excellent. This is partly because of the Dead Assassin and his gruesome makeup effects, but mostly because the art design mockups of the location are like nothing I've ever seen. Every green on Earth dangles and shimmers like a tapestry reflected in the water. Camouflaged monstrosities crawl in and out of the mud, while Spanish Moss hangs from a canopy like giant teeth. It's a death metal masterpiece.

Ben Schilling, Leon, and I are having a good time in our own way. I'm running rehearsals, unsupervised, and we spend most of our time laughing, sharing stories, and comparing tattoos. I'm particularly fond of the scorpion tattoo on Schilling's left forearm. It's wearing sunglasses and a sombrero, holding a Corona between its pincers, yet it somehow manages to be terrifying.

Despite his prolific performing experience, Ben Schilling is not a great mover. He's always trying to rush through choreography, forgetting to drop his hips, and I continually remind him that "slow is smooth, smooth is fast." We break down each move into five or six micro-movements to get his body used to the mechanics. Schilling enjoys the training process. I give a lot of leadership to Leon in an effort to build their relationship as partners. The goal is to get Schilling to hire the two of us on future projects and bolster our careers. He explains to us how glad he is to have these rehearsals, since usually he's just brought on set to do his scenes without any time allotted for experimentation. It's clear that Ben Schilling loves being in a creative space, and he even brings Leon and me gifts of chocolate and mezcal (which I don't drink).

Halona and I are still texting, although I have no idea why. I feel nothing for her. My heart is a cold, sleeping octopus. Perhaps I'm too proud to think about Halona. And I should be! No one, including myself would ever believe I could earn two paychecks and not convert them directly into eight-balls and expensive whiskey. That's magic right there. That's real-life movie magic.

Wolfblood gets better, almost to her full health.

But then she eats another rat and gets even sicker. *"Much, much worse,"* according to Aurora. Now, in a clearer state of mind, I'm able to look up 'botulism' online, and it turns out it isn't caused by eating poisoned rats. I don't know what kind of donkey-fuck veterinarian Aurora went to, but anyone with a laptop can diagnose rodenticide toxicosis. I tell her to immediately discontinue the antitoxin injections, and to stand by because I'm coming to save the cat.

At the end of three weeks, with the previzes finished, we have a Monday off, so I fly to New York to rescue Wolfblood, my soul apart from my body.

I leave the sleeping octopus in New Orleans, because New York in the summertime is my wheelhouse. My zombie playpen. I'm going to make sure Wolfblood is OK, and then I might allow myself to have some beers at my old spots, because it's summertime, and I fucking deserve it.

My dreams on the plane are terrible.

I'm swimming in a wide, shallow sea. The pale, sandy floor is clear and unobstructed, just like the sunlight. But I'm not just swimming. I'm journeying toward Wolfblood, who I find floating on her back in the middle of the ocean. When I finally reach her, she's enormous. I climb onto her body like a shipwreck survivor and collapse on top of her, exhausted. Bloody is despondent and helpless, legs splayed in four directions. She can't speak, but only looks at me. I say the few words she understands: "sweetie," and "I love you," and "good kitty kitty."

She hugs me, and this makes me even sadder and causes us to roll over into the water, only it's not the ocean anymore. It's my bed in New York. The one Aurora's sleeping in right now.

Now, Aurora is on top of me, and I love her too. But Wolfblood is gone, and I want her back, so I roll hard with Aurora back the other direction. It doesn't work, and now I'm on top of Aurora on the other side of the bed. Muffled sounds of Harlem drift around us.

"We had fun together," Aurora says, somberly. "All those years on tour." Her silvery eyes glimmer up at me.

"Yeah," I say, my heart sinking fast. I'm missing Wolfblood, although Aurora kind of *feels* like Bloody, somehow. "We had a lot of good times. A lot of years."

"We've known each other for *eighteen years,*" she says, and the enormity in her expression forces me to reel. "I loved you, Lex."

"I know."

"But I never *really* loved you. I mean . . . because of Jake. Now I'm fading away, and I've never really loved . . . anyone."

A tear wells up in my eye, spills over and drops. It feels more like bleeding than crying. The tear lands in Aurora's eye, causing her to blink. Then she sneezes in my face. But somehow it doesn't spoil the moment. We look at each other for what feels like the end of an album. She has a flushed, electrified look on her face from the sneeze.

Then, slowly, she opens her mouth. It opens wider, much too wide, and the air suddenly fills with a rancid, rotten cat's breath smell. Her eyes start to bulge, which causes me to stop crying immediately. Fear wedges its way into my chest. Aurora's silvery blue irises flood the whites of her eyes and turn furry, like slimy newborn kittens squirming in her orbitals.

Then she screams.

The plane jostles gently, and I wake up. Aurora's screams have blended into the dull whine of the ventilation system.

Visions and emotions swarm my heart like ghosts. I press the flight attendant button, instinctively summoning a drink.

A chubby Latina woman with nice breasts arrives, smiling, and says, "Did you need something, hun?" She un-lights the call button.

I take a slow breath. "Just a coffee, please. Black." I look down and check my wardrobe. Black sweats. Black sweatshirt. Leather vest. I'm doing OK. I suffered the thirst until I got used to it. I climbed the wretched mountain alone, and now I'm gonna sit up here for a while where the air is pure and crisp.

"Coffee black," she says. "You got it."

Eventually we touch down.

I give the chubby stewardess my phone number and get in an Uber. No checked baggage this time. Just a backpack.

By the time I get to my apartment I've already decided that I'm not going to call any of my friends. And I'm not going to drink anything. Fuck everybody. I'm not even going to ride my motorcycle.

What I *am* going to do is cuddle with Bloody on the bed for two days. Aurora can sleep next to us if she wants.

I will not text Halona.

It feels good putting keys into old familiar locks and opening familiar doors into familiar smells. But not that good. The fire hydrant out front splatters great arches of water into the street. Kids play and scream. Adults drink large cans of micheladas around carts with rainbow parasols. Dominican dub step blares from car stereos, as the sun goes down over Harlem.

Aurora's not home, and my dark apartment makes me thirsty. Whoever's mind hotel I inhabit is an alcoholic. It still smells like a bar in here, even a month after I left.

Aurora has two suitcases underneath the breakfast bar, lying open. Aside from that and the bricolage of toiletries filling up my tiny bathroom, my apartment looks the same as ever, with the same ominous, dim light.

Wolfblood is on the bed, just as I knew she would be. She's lying on her side, not curled up, trying to keep her belly cool in the hot room. I turn on the air conditioner, mentally scolding Aurora for not leaving it on, and curl up on the bed beside her. Bloody purrs in loud, rapid bursts, but otherwise doesn't move. The party music outside vibrates my bed, somehow making the moment even sadder.

"Bloody," I whisper. "My girl."

She purrs louder.

After fifteen minutes in the bed with Wolfblood, I'm struck with an inspiration, followed by a clear idea. I sit up, stroke Bloody a few times, then leave the room. There's something I have to do before it gets fully dark.

I put on my boots and head back downstairs. Maria, my neighbor, is in the hallway. When she sees me, she freezes, and her dark eyes go huge. She steps out of my way, puts her back to the wall, and raises her hand to her chest. Her fingers move, and I realize she's crossing herself minutely, hoping I don't see it.

Maria thinks I'm dead.

"Maria," I say, "que tal. No soy muerte." I should smile at this, but I can't.

She starts to tremble, as if the Grim Reaper is lurching toward her down the hall. "Dio," she whispers, trying to keep her knees from buckling.

"I'm OK," I say. I manage to slow down a little, and when she sees my face closer up, she leavens. Not much— she still has a wide-eyed rabbit look—but she stops shaking and says, "Mister Mercier?"

I realize that Maria is seeing something she's never seen before. Me, with color in my face and light in my eyes, sober and fully upright. "Yes. Hi," I say. "I've been working out of town."

She doesn't believe me. She does believe in ghosts, however, as most Dominicans do. She probably thinks that when drunk people die, their ghosts emerge clear-eyed and fresh-looking, as if hangovers can't cross the River Styx.

"I need to ask you something." I stop my approach, holding out my hands. "My cat is very sick. She's not moving much. Are there other pets in the building that are sick? Like, cats?"

Maria breaks eye contact with me long enough to think. "Si," she says. "Two cats. They die this week." She's wringing the hem of her blouse. "And two last week."

"Fucking hell!" I'm not masking my horror at all. "For real? De verdad?"

Maria lets out a breath, finally mollifying a little. She's not afraid of me anymore, but she is still amazed. "Yes," she says.

"Why?" I say. "How? Four cats in two weeks? What's happening?"

Maria explains that the rats are out of control this summer, so the superintendent started poisoning them. This is what I had feared. The rats are all fleeing to the second and third floors with arsenic in their blood. And the resident cats, diligently called to arms to defend their homes, are dying on the battlefield like Native Americans with poisoned turkey in their guts on Thanksgiving.

Rage explodes in me like startled pigeons. I turn around and rush back into my apartment, tossing a weak "gracias" over my shoulder as I go.

There's a veterinary clinic in Washington Heights that's open late. Wolfblood and I have been there many times. I call them and explain the situation. When they agree to see us, I grab my motorcycle and lug it out into the freight elevator, then onto the street.

Outside, the grownups all cease their conversations and stare at me, unbelieving. One man throws his head back and laughs.

Returning to my apartment, I retrieve Wolfblood's Sherpa bag from the closet. I'm not thinking clearly. Calling an Uber would be the right thing to do, because Amsterdam is a truck route, and it's full of potholes and trucks, and it's loud as hell. Wolfblood hates being on my bike, especially on that treacherous road to the vet. But I have tunnel vision, and Ubers and phone apps are not within the tunnel.

I gently put Wolfblood into her carrier and sling it over my shoulder. My goal is not only to get her some anti-poison (if that's even a thing), but also to get her rabies vaccine, along with all the paperwork necessary to allow her to fly to New Orleans with me. The Wollcroft is a pet-friendly hotel, and I mean to be with Wolfblood for the rest of the run.

If I can't get her paperwork, I'll ride with her on my Harley the whole way to New Orleans. I'll leave tomorrow morning before the dawn. I'll bring all her favorite toys, and I'll buy a litter box when I get there.

Trucks thunder past us at deafening speed. Wolfblood squalls the whole way. It's 8:30 p.m., and people and cars are everywhere. A yellow cab cuts us off at 156th Street, causing me to brake so hard my back tire slides sideways. I almost drop the bike, but adrenaline forces me to stamp my left leg into the pavement. The Chrome Dragon rights itself, but I blow out my left leg completely, and I know I won't be walking right for a week—a month, if I pulled a hamstring. But I don't think about that now, and I can't feel it anyways, because I'm on a track.

Stumbling through the vet clinic doors I shout, "I'm Lex Mercier!" Then Aurora texts me. I also have four hundred and three unread texts on the "Frankenstein Stuntarinos" text thread.

Aurora says, *Umm. . . I'm home, and I can't find Wolfblood. . . or your bike. Were you here?*

Was I there!? Of course I was there!

The vet receptionist sets us up, and I'm barely able to mask the avalanche of rage that's happening just behind my face, somehow getting Bloody and myself into an examination room.

I text Aurora back, stroking Wolfblood as we wait.

I'm at the vet with Bloody.

Four cats died in the building.

Poison rats. The fucking Super. Rats go crazy. The cats eat them and die. I'm looking for anti-poison.

Save yourself.

Wolfblood passes her exams, and we get the papers we need to fly together. I call Delta Airlines immediately and give them one hundred dollars and a promise to keep my animal in the footwell at all times during the flight. The veterinarian is sympathetic and soft. She coos when she speaks. She gives me Atropine tablets for the poison, as well as activated charcoal, and vitamin K. She explains that it's a long shot, but there's a chance it might help.

When I exit the vet clinic, I realize I'm tingling, but I can't tell if it's from rage, or fear, or just mild panic from being back in New York. There's a rose garden outside the building, so I break a rose off and reenter the clinic, finding Bloody's vet, and handing her the rose.

"Is that from our garden?" she says.

"Yes. I'm sorry. I didn't know what to do. I think you saved Bloody's life. I'm very grateful." I start to say thank you, but my throat swells up, and I can't. Instead, I turn my back to her and limp away, feeling slightly better.

Bloody is accustomed to flying with me. She was with me when I left New York for Los Angeles ten years ago, and she was with me when I moved back to New York last year to work on *The Lesser Dead* series, which wrapped five months before *Everyone's Frankenstein* started up. During those flights Wolfblood was calm, and she never showcased any catlike overreactions. This time she's her same agreeable self, and she sleeps in my lap the whole flight. A little girl in a *Stranger Things* T-shirt sits next to us, and she helps me pet Bloody when my arms get tired.

I don't sleep on the flight, and I don't dream.

People move out of our way, as we limp through Louis Armstrong International, determination stamped all over us. My leg feels terrible, and Bloody is getting restless. When we get outside, I hear one guy say to his wife, "*Dang*, I ain't been this hot since frickin' Florida!"

As soon as we get in an Uber, the rain begins to fall.

I don't speak to the driver on the way to the Wollcroft, and I never check my phone for messages. My eyes stay on

Wolfblood the whole ride, while my hands never stop gliding through her fur. Bloody isn't purring anymore because the rain is loud, and there are lots of bumps. Also she purred throughout the whole flight, and I bet that gets tiring after a while. She does come out of her carrier and walk around the back seat. The Uber driver doesn't appear to mind. I would surely give him an earful if he did.

When I see Miss Jenny at the front desk, I must look tired because she gives me a sympathetic sway and says, "Mr. Mercier, where *have* you been?"

"I've been in New York," I say, gesturing behind me at the glass doors. "Picked up my cat. This is Bloody." I hold up the Sherpa bag. "That's Miss Jenny, girl. She's a *friend*."

"Well, it's been a crazy weekend," Miss Jenny says. "Lotta your folks been having fun, that's all I'm gonna say."

Wolfblood and I spend a quiet night in. It's still early on Monday, so I'm able to go out and get a litter box and some other gear.

Bloody likes the hotel room. I set up her food dishes near the fridge on the floor, and I sneak some Atropine into her wet food, telling her it's "Southern cuisine." Wolfblood doesn't eat the food, but she walks around it for a while, investigating.

After a shower I fall into bed and pull out my phone. Six hundred and twenty "Frankenstein Stuntarinos" text messages, and none of them are important except for the call sheet, which I screenshot. Eventually, Wolfblood climbs onto the bed and curls up over my left ankle in her usual spot. She's purring again, but now there's an extra chirp, a high-pitched bird-like whirring in her throat, which causes me to fantasize about disappearing into a K-hole, black and bottomless, sparkling, and pervasive.

"Good night, Bloody my love."

She whaps her tail.

I slip into my usual jerky twitches. My legs piston in and out of reality. Wolfblood is used to it. I kick, she bucks. Sometimes my restless leg syndrome goes full body.

Eventually I stop glitching, and we both sleep.

My dreams are plenty, and they're not good.

I imagine Wolfblood's dreams have poison in them.

GUNS IN HOTEL ROOMS

BACK IN ON Tuesday for more previz.

We arrive late, grumpily pushing ourselves through the steel door into Stage C. It's five minutes to eight, and when we walk in Leon's in mid-air throwing a front flip and catching two pistols, landing in a perfect crouch with both guns leveled, aiming at Jin and Cripple. They cheer, and Jin shouts, "Bro, that was fucking disgusting." They all high-five each other.

I dump my stunt bag on top of a flight case and take a slow, desultory sip of coffee, then lumber onto the mat. Sadie, in a center split rocking back and forth says, "What's up, Lex! How was your weekend?"

"Hey," I say, plopping down next to her. "I'm late for work, and I really hate being late."

"It's seven fifty-five!"

"No, I'm late. I'm always thirty minutes early. Now I'm all out of sorts."

"Oh," she says. "I'm sorry about that. So why are you late?"

"I got a goddamn ticket."

"For what? Speeding?" Sadie retracts her legs from the split position and starts massaging her own shoulder.

"No. For putting a quarter into someone else's parking meter."

"That's illegal?"

"Yes, Sadie, that's illegal. It's a fucking crime! Do you believe this? I got a ticket right in front of the hotel, on the way to the parking structure. It was embarrassing, Miss Jenny saw me."

"Oh, damn, dude."

"The officer's name was Fuck-Piss."

"Really?"

"No, I made that part up. I just want this to have a happy ending."

"Damn," Sadie says again. Then she considers something. "Hey, why was Miss Jenny there? Doesn't she work nights?"

"She got promoted," I say. "She's a manager now. She's gonna be working days."

"Awesome!"

"Yeah, I'm stoked. Is Fury here yet?"

"Fury is everywhere!" Target shouts. He's practicing kicks with Pit Mix.

I tap my phone, which is lying on the mat next to me. It's 8:01.

We're starting the swamp scene today. I'm feeling pretty good about it, despite my sprained left leg and my limp. I'll just tell them I dropped my bike, and they'll think that's really cool.

Other things try to mar me, dare to disarm me. The late start, the embarrassing ticket from Officer Fuck-Piss, Wolfblood's mostly limp and lifeless body.

But I'm here now, and I'm ready to shred. This is the Dead Assassin's scene, goddammit, and I'm ready to howl at the stars. I'm gonna kick and scream the day away, and I'm gonna enjoy it.

Fall down once, get up twice.

Let's fucking go. As they say.

When Fury arrives, the whole room busies into a mad aviary. We're building boxes and tossing them everywhere while the riggers hang span sets and roll their genies around. A few pieces of truss are bolted together to make a tree, some kind of giant oak that erupts out of the middle of the swamp like the Tree of Life in some grimy dark paradise. I've seen the photos and drawings. The location is awesome. Southern Gothic to the metal power. Absolutely gorgeous.

But for the meantime we're throwing cardboard boxes around, and the room looks like an 8-bit Minecraft popcorn machine, until Fury shouts, "Alright guys, let's bring it in!"

Everyone drifts over to Ed. If we were in canoes, we'd be caught in an eddy, har-har.

Fury talks us through the scene, and when he gets to the part where the Dead Assassin shows up, Leon raises his hand and says, "Do we know who's playing the Dead Assassin?"

Fury sticks his hands in his pockets. I'm surprised they fit. "Well," he says, "Morley wants Lex."

Everyone cheers, "Lex!" except for Fury, who just stands there, allowing it, and Pit Mix, who looks up startled and says, "What happened?"

After the talk-through, I go into the costume shop to find Zelda. It's attached to the stunt gym, remember. I ask Zelda if I can borrow one of the capes for the previz. She tells me no, I can't use the cape for the previz. So I go back into the stunt gym, stopping in the unused kitchen that connects the two rooms so I can vape some nicotine.

The swamp fight goes like this:

We remember from the opening, while Frankenstein's monster was learning to read and write, that the farmer who nurtured him had found Doctor Frankenstein's laboratory notes. These notes turned out to be crucial, even after the farmer died.

The cottage was in ruins. Only a smoking foundation and a lone, flagstone chimney. A couple of graverobbers on their way to the nearby cemetery decided to stop at the cottage and scrounge around, hoping to find some old valuables buried in the ashes.

What they found was Doctor Frankenstein's laboratory notes.

Cut to one hundred years later. The lab notes have been sold and traded. Experiments were carried out by a group of scientists way out in the remote bayou, hidden within the foggy swamps. These laboratories are nothing more than house boats. From the outside they look like small, scattered construction trailers floating on pontoons.

There, the monsters come. Created in the dark swamps, under mossy oaks and bearded sycamores that loom like giant hands casting magic spells over the bog, in the murky gloom they wander.

Graves are carelessly robbed. Bodies are punctured by shovels and coarsely stitched together with leather laces before their reanimation. The ghouls that seem brainless are cast out to roam the swamps, which are vast but contained, a dark world of its own.

Meanwhile, Frankenstein's monster, being intelligent, had copied the laboratory notes for himself. This was just before he smothered the farmer and his wife with the balcony and then hurled his flaming body at the oil tank. Frank has since conducted his own experiments, in an effort to find love and obtain a bride.

Frankenstein is walking through the bayou with one of his bride hopeful atrocities when he is attacked by the evil scientists and their horde of undead leviathans.

A huge fight ensues. Bodies are dashed against trees, run over by boats, and every time a creature is smashed into something it explodes in a cinematic red cloud of bone and gristle.

Eventually the Dead Assassin appears. He's the mad scientist's pride project. Rather than cast his idiot zombie to the swamps, this man had kept it. He taught it to speak and to think, much like Dr. Frankenstein's original monster. Everyone's Frankenstein, right? This scientist is the fool of the scene, and he dies a gruesome death, getting thrown through the window of his houseboat, landing hard on the pontoon with his head in the water while the heedless creatures swarm him and drag his flailing body, along with the entire houseboat, underwater.

The Dead Assassin kills Frankenstein's bride hopeful by braining her against a mossy stump. Frankenstein flinches at this, heartbroken at first, then enraged.

A stand-off ensues between Frank and the Dead Assassin. Ben Schilling's gonna say some Academy Award-winning lines, and then our fight begins. I say a few lines to Schilling as well. One of them is actually pretty juicy. It comes later in the fight, and it goes like this:

DEAD ASSASSIN:
There is rage in me, the likes of which no man should ever endure. And there is strength in you, dear Alpha. But strength is no contest . . . for pure black *rage!*

Really good stuff.

After a long and bloody battle, Frankenstein creams the Dead Assassin in the tenth round. We're on top of a slanted, half-sunken houseboat, and I manage to pin him onto his stomach with his eyeball squared over a jutting shard of glass. He's struggling for his life, staring at the shard as it gets closer, closer. This is where I say my line. When he hears the word "rage," the shard punctures his eyeball, spurting black blood all over the camera lens. Frankenstein screams and throws an elbow, staggering me backwards. But as he stands up and spins to face me, I blast him in the face with an uppercut, sending him flipping and twirling into the air, landing lifelessly on the slanted roof, sliding down into the swamp, and sinking to the bottom.

My face twists into an evil "told you so" grin, and I turn my back to the empty water where Frankenstein disappeared.

But it turns out my words weren't true. Strength *is* a match for pure black rage. Behind me Frankenstein emerges slowly from the water. One eye is gushing blood and clogged with mud, and he's dragging a huge canoe out of the swamp. It's clotted with moss and vines, and it looks heavy. I'm facing the camera, so only the audience can see what's rearing up behind me. Frankenstein brings the boat down like he's mauling firewood. *Smash!* The boat crushes me. Blood bursts all over the sunken pontoon trailer while Frankenstein reloads. *Smash!* He does it again, then a fourth time, until there's nothing left in the water but bubbles and blood and floating sticks that used to be the houseboat.

It takes seven days to shoot the previz, but we get it.

We end early on the seventh day, and everyone tells me what a good actor I am, and we celebrate with a production-paid lunch at Let's Pho.

I arrive humbly and sit down next to Leon, who appears hungover and sweaty. His knees are wiggling a lot, and I pretend I don't mind.

Ed Fury is telling one of his stories, and the stunt team is leaning into him hungrily. Something about a kid who accidently punched him in the face on the last *Fast and Furious* movie, resulting in Fury kicking all the kid's teeth in during the subsequent take, sending him to the hospital. I've seen Fury proud of himself before, but not this proud. The story is awful, and it doesn't merit the arrogant gestures he makes while telling it. I can tell that the stunt team doesn't know how to react, so I decide chime in, feeling cavalier after my fine performance.

"Dude, one time this stunt guy kept swinging a shovel too close to my face," I say. "Like, I had to fade all the way back to holding to avoid getting hit. I kept telling this guy to choke up, stop aiming for my face, you know? But he kept doing it! So, I stole his laptop."

No one speaks. It's like they're all being tested, solving for x, and no one wants to be wrong.

"I gave it back to him the next day."

"What show was that?" Fury asks.

"Locke and Key."

"That's not a real show."

After lunch, Cripple gets in the van with Leon and me, and he shows us the swamp fight previz. Cripple doesn't speak much in general, but when he does it's little more than a nasal, smoky whisper. He's always pushing his glasses up on his nose like a child. But despite his meek voice and glasses, Cripple is a blockade of a man. A total athletic thud.

The previz is good. However, "Sweet Child o' Mine" is the music, which triggers me, almost to the point of punching the laptop screen. Instead, I grind my teeth and squeeze the steering wheel. The whole thing is ruined. Anything would've been better than "Sweet Child o' Mine." Why not something cold and dark like Carcass, or Tragedy? Or even some Hans Zimmer score from the *Batman* trilogy. These kids have no fucking sensibilities. No culture.

No doubt Fury loves it. It's as sterile and pastel as his Instagram sponsorships. Also, it's pitch-perfect within today's nineties infatuation. Ed Fury loves being current. I mean, look at how tight his pants are.

And yes, I know, "Sweet Child o' Mine" is eighties, not nineties. But somehow, it's been lumped into the whole nineties thing, and whatever, I don't fucking care. Our childhood is precious, but it isn't meant to be canonized or made permanent. The music that made me who I am is now the soundtrack to a stupid fight rehearsal. My life is a joke because I'm old and I'm realizing it too late.

"I'm not supposed to be here," I whisper, massaging my forehead. No one does, so I say, louder this time, "What's up with the music?"

"It's Guns N' Roses," Cripple says, from the passenger seat.

"I know it's Guns N' Roses. What's it doing in the swamp scene?"

"What do you mean?" he says. "It's fucking dope."

"Yeah, it's dope," Leon says from the backseat. "It's retro, dude."

"Retro is *never* dope," I say, dropping my face into my hands, which smell faintly of pork belly.

"Well," Cripple says, "Jin did the music. I do the editing and the after-effects. Jin does the music and sound effects." He slides his laptop into his bag resignedly, then adjusts his glasses on his nose.

"It's not right," I say.

"I think it's dope," Leon reiterates.

I raise my face from my hands. The clouds are melting, and a light rain starts to fall. The trees that surround the parking lot sway gently. The rest of the team is gone, and the parking lot is now empty. "I'm sorry, Cripple," I say. "The previz is amazing. Really good work. I'm sorry. I'm just tired."

Thoughtful silence.

"You want a ride to the Wollcroft?"

"Sure, bro," Cripple says. "Let me throw my One-Wheel in the back if that's OK."

"Can we stop for a smoothie?" Leon says.

"Of course."

There's a pause.

"Are you sure you're OK, Lex? You look kind of sick." Cripple adjusts his glasses again, looking very young and put together.

"I'm fine," I say, turning the ignition and starting the van. "My throat is scratchy, that's all. And my cat is sick. And I'm tired. And I hate Guns N' Roses."

"I thought you loved Guns N' Roses!" Leon says from the back seat.

"Well, I guess I did," I say. "I mean, I don't think I do anymore. It sucks because I know every song of theirs by heart." I accidentally see my pale, pathetic face in the rear-view mirror and quickly look away. "I was obsessed with them as a child."

"A *sweet* child?" Leon says.

"Yeah, sure. But now they're just . . . I don't know, *old*. Their music is like a bad memory. Their energy is dead. They're like an old girlfriend I don't want to fuck anymore. Now they're just . . . gross."

"Hey, that's OK," Cripple says. "Good metaphor, by the way. Maybe it's because now they're *retro*."

"But what if metal becomes retro?" I plead. "What do I do then?"

Cripple thinks about this. "Well, people are wearing Slayer shirts now."

"Yeah, Slayer shirts are in, bro," Leon agrees.

"That's different, guys. No one's actually playing Slayer's music. You should put 'Hell Awaits' over the fucking swamp fight. But of course, you won't. Because it's not cool."

"Come on, Lex, you're overreacting," Cripple says.

"I know." I close my eyes. "I'm sorry."

The minivan is quiet for a while, as the rain clatters on the roof. Then I get an idea. "Hey guys, can we stop at District Donuts for a coffee? I want to look at the cashier's tits for a few minutes."

"Of course," Cripple says. "Whatever you need."

"Yeah, we got you," Leon agrees.

Back at the Wollcroft, I'm slumped on the edge of the bed, staring at the rain ripples in the pool. It's midafternoon and the courtyard is empty. Nothingness glistens like snake leather. The window is slanted open, and a warm breeze wafts in, and although I find it all beautiful, this is as far outside as I want to go, barring cigarette breaks. Wolfblood wheezes at the foot of the bed, while *The Virgin Suicides* narration floods the room with fumes of beautiful depression, reminding me that the last one to die is always ourselves.

I text Halona again, but I don't know why. We've been texting for five weeks, building up nothing. I imagine how small she'd look in a foreign city, her silhouette framed between Chinaberry trees, feet crooked on the cobblestone. I can hear her intuitive questions that perhaps I might need to be asked at this point. Women are good for that. There's something at work in my soul that I don't understand.

I can smell her gardenia shampoo and vodka tonics, and that is what makes me tingle with the recognition that there's a center in me, an invariable place called home, and I am far from it.

Midafternoon, and my room is dark, even with the curtains open. Warm buckets of jasmine-scented air flow through the window like a slow heartbeat.

I pause *The Virgin Suicides,* because I can't write a text to Halona and listen to a book at the same time.

Hey girl! I'm ready for that physical therapy [smiley face] *My back feels like hot garbage. Offer still open?*

The only sound now is the rain. I look toward Wolfblood at the foot of the bed, and for the first time in weeks she's lying on her back instead of her side, a sign of better comfort. The infections must be clearing from her body. I lean sideways, causing the bed to creak sluggishly, and run my fingertips through the fur of her belly. She squeaks a little, then continues purring.

My phone buzzes. I sit back up.

Halona: *Of course, babe! What's your schedule look like?*

Myself: *We start filming next week, and it's gonna be crazy, but the week after should be pretty light.*

Halona: *How much longer are you out there?*

Myself: *Five weeks. Maybe less if they don't need me for the last scene. It's driving stuff, but my boss doesn't trust me with a car.*

Halona: *Why not? lol*

Myself: *Because he thinks I'm dangerous. He's probably right.*

I don't add the obvious reasoning that I already spilled cocaine all over one of his rentals.

Halona: *I don't have any clients from 8/4 – 8/10*

Myself: *Perfect! I'll set you up with a flight.*

Halona: *Sweet!!*

Myself: *Send me your full name, date of birth, and seat prefer-ence, and I'll get back to you with the info. Woot!*

It's very quiet in my room, while Halona doesn't re-spond. My mind is quiet too, which is rare, and kind of nice. Then I hear a scream, followed by a splash, which causes me to look back at the pool. Two girls are out there in the rain. One is treading water, telling the other how warm it is. The second girl jumps in, pinching her nose for comic effect. When she hits the water, she's swallowed by the bubbling surface and disappears from my view. I envy that. I wish I could disappear in the rain. But I don't want to go outside. Instead, I turn to look at my fridge. There's still food in there from five weeks ago.

My phone lights up, but it's not Halona. It would have vibrated if it were. It's Cripple, posting something on the "Frankenstein Stuntarinos" text thread, which is set to "do not disturb." Unread text, number six hundred sixty-three. I open it, because I'm not thinking.

What appears is a video.

Cautiously, I press play.

Laughter shrieks from my Bluetooth speaker, where *The Virgin Suicides* was soothing me only minutes before.

Cripple is sitting on his bed by the window, exactly where I'm sitting now but in a different room. Pit Mix is in there, and it looks like Jin is taking the video, because when Cripple says, "What do you keep in your bedside table?" I hear Jin say, "Hard drives and stuff. What about you?" and then Cripple opens his nightstand and pulls out a black AR

Pistol with a folded butt stock. In one swift movement he draws the gun, flips the butt stock open with a 'click' and shoulders it, low-ready. They all laugh.

I look out my window at the two girls who are doing handstands in the swimming pool. It's getting dark. Inside my mind hotel, it's dark in the daytime, and when it becomes night, it's as black and cold as fucking Guinness. I'm so thirsty right now. I've been thirsty for five weeks, and I haven't gotten used to it yet. I am ungrateful. I've been working, learning, and creating with two of the greatest performers of all time. Ben Schilling and Leon fucking Williams. But all I can think about is the growing void in my heart, and the supplicating need for cold foam in my stomach, and warmth, and tenderness.

And now it's nighttime again. I'm glad I have that bag of cocaine in the Excedrin bottle in the bathroom. Because somehow that makes it my choice. I'm not forced into sobriety. I choose to be like this. It's mine.

I choose to be like this.

I stand up harshly and walk over all the dirty clothes that are crusting between the window and the bed, stopping once to kiss Bloody's belly. Then I float over to the bathroom and open the Excedrin bottle. I pull out the little plastic bag, hold it up to my nose, and smell the power of it. It's probably fifteen seconds before my phone buzzes again, shunting me out of my trance.

Halona, that's right! I have a secret friend, and she's coming here to see me. I *will* find warmth and tenderness, after all.

Halona Jones, what a name. In one second, I've already come up with a song about her, and a film, both of which are titled *Halona Jones*. She was born in two thousand two. That makes her only twenty-one years old. Young enough to be my stepdaughter from a much younger wife. My pants tighten in a pleasing way.

I tell Halona I'm on it like white on coke, and to expect an itinerary soon. I also explain that there might be days when I'm at work for twelve hours or more, and that she should enjoy the city while I'm out trashing it, but she can also hang out in the hotel or do whatever she wants.

The phone lights up again, but it's not Halona. It's more "Stuntarinos" bullshit.

Mike, the head rigger, has made a video of his own. It's a POV shot of himself walking across his hotel room to the cabinet in the bathroom where the towels are kept. He removes a small stack of white towels and draws an Uzi from the back of the cubby. He racks the gun using his phone hand, causing the image to spaz for a second, then spins around and aims it at the front door, where there's a map of the hotel floor plan. Then he idles, like a video game character.

I expect there's more of this coming, remembering how Target had asked me to take care of all the guns in his hotel room while he went to Atlanta for the weekend. (I just fostered them in my room so the hotel staff wouldn't stumble upon them unexpectedly.)

A moment later, a video from Target arrives.

Smiling to myself, I press play, realizing I'm having a lot of fun looking at these things.

Another POV. In this one Target approaches his door from outside in the hallway, swipes his card key and enters the room, stumbling directly to his microwave, opening it, and pulling out a Glock nine-millimeter. He swivels to the left, opens his freezer, and tosses the Glock into the ice tray. Beside the ice tray is a flamethrower with a can of gasoline screwed into the side. I remember Target telling me that he had patented his own flamethrower, and there it is, in the freezer. He pushes the camera in to the "flame" icon painted on the gas can, then pulls out, slams the freezer door, and opens the fridge, revealing a large, expensive-looking rifle. The model is unfamiliar to me, too chunky to be a tactical carbine, and too short for a sniper rifle. It fits diagonally in the fridge, which has had its shelves removed, leaning next to a bottle of ketchup and some scattered soy sauce packets.

Nothing I've written in this story is true, except for this:

Target Hinman is a genius. I don't know how he does it, but he seems to be consistently happy, every day. I mean, happiness is the goal of life, right? Some would disagree and say that *love* is the meaning of life, that happiness isn't real unless it's shared. Well, Target has that too. A wife, and a beautiful young boy back home in Atlanta. But Target's constant affability is infectious. His joy is catching, even though he's kind of a monster and an asshole in other ways. Target's a bleeding-heart Republican, the kind that believes all Democrats are demons, and he sells and manufactures firearms. He watches fail videos that become deaths. He invests in crypto currency, idolizes Elon Musk, often says dumber shit than me . . .

And I fucking love him.

Leon uses his genius to do double side-flips. What is he even thinking? He needs to hang out with Target more.

My phone buzzes again. This time it's Cripple, on a private com.

We're going to Barcadia in 20 minutes. Come with us.

I look out the window, where a hard summer rain hammers darkness into everything. A ghost of a smile touches the corner of my mouth.

Halona texts me back.

Sweet!!!

ACCIDENTAL DARKNESS

FUCK THIS SHIT.

Fuck all this useless, sanctimonious, sober bullshit.

As I wade through a sea of college girls at Barcadia (three hundred of them, all wearing more or less the same outfit), I feel a brimming sense of hope that tonight is going to be the most auspicious drunk of my life.

The crowd parts before me, revealing an aisle that leads to a beacon of light that is the bar.

Artless dance remixes of nineties alternative music rattle the walls, and a kind of myopic confusion stirs the crowd into a directionless current. I can smell all the Keratin treatments and shampoos as my head floats over the crowd and lands squarely in front of the bartender's face. The only face in the building that knows what it's doing.

"Double Sazerac and a lager, please."

Behind me, and to either side is an avalanche of sound. Garrulous women are yelling, three hundred movies playing at the same time.

"What kind of lager?" he says.

"Don't kill my buzz, man. Just a lager."

He looks confused for a second, then turns and swishes off to do the Lord's work. I turn around as well, resting my back against the bar and removing my sunglasses. Colored lights pulse over the crowd in branches. Everyone's a redhead for a second, then a blonde, now purple heads and it looks like a computer simulation because all the hairstyles are the same, a thin white line of scalp going right up the middle of young heads, while Red Hot Chili Peppers gets raped by eighth notes.

My back is feeling better because of the shot of CBD I drank before getting dressed, and I notice one girl looking at me with a wary, almost fearful expression, while another one gives me a hungry vulpine smile, and a quote from *Frankenstein* flashes behind my eyes like neon: "How mutable are our feelings, and how strange is that clinging love we have of life, even in the excess of misery."

Or something like that.

Fake Chili Peppers segues into fake Guns N' Roses—a soulless reimagining of "Sweet Child o' Mine," which causes me to whirl around and ask the bartender what his problem is, and why he wants to torture me so bad, and if he was raised by tortoises. But when I turn around, he's there, smiling but looking worried at the same time. My two drinks are right in front of me.

"That's a Faubourg Lager," he says. "And a double Sazerac."

"You're the man," I tell him. "How much?"

Cripple, Jin, Sadie, Target, and Pit Mix are in the back room, where the music's even louder. They're excited to start filming on Monday, and doubly proud of the previzes we've all completed on schedule. Everything is lined up and unobstructed.

But I don't immediately head into the back room. Not yet. I'm going to stand here and drink this Sazerac first. And then order another one.

The more I drink, the better that white's gonna feel later.

I raise the Sazerac up to my nose and breathe it in. The minty, apothecary aroma causes a shudder in my chest, reminding me of all those innocent weeks I suffered at work and in the hotel room. I suddenly feel small. I can see myself slumped on the side of my bed, unable to sleep, watching the pool with dirty laundry by my feet, not eating, worrying about Wolfblood while trying to entertain myself with audiobooks. The hair on the back of my neck is standing up. Something feels wrong. I'm being warned.

I'm surprised to find myself like this. I've never had a beer I didn't enjoy.

I stare at the glass of whiskey and the beer, suddenly a stranger to it all, realizing that yes, I'm thirsty and I want a belly full of cold foam more than anything. But do I really need to go down this road? I know where it leads. It's nothing new. It leads to a pathetic Saturday, followed by another thirty years of headaches and predictable mood swings. It leads to the same old Lex. And hasn't life been more productive lately? Fresher? More honest? The stunt team seems to trust me a lot more, and likewise, I'm trusting myself.

I'm trusting myself. That's the bottom line.

I struggle with these thoughts for what feels like a long time. By the time fake G N' R merges into fake Oasis I reach an epiphany, realizing that although my life is full of anguish and pain—with twenty-six broken bones and thirteen spinal herniations, a gashed-up leg and torso, two missing toes and four missing teeth—my life still remains dear to me, and I will defend it. And I'll not pickle it with Sazerac and stomach aches, and all the girls in the club suddenly cheer for some reason, causing me to take a step backwards from the bar. Now from a few feet away, the drinks are nothing more than fake movie decorations, and my mind is suddenly clear. I have my strength again.

I visualize Wolfblood thanking me with wise, tequila-colored eyes.

I slide my sunglasses back onto my face and turn away from the bar, bumping into a girl who looks like she's about twelve. She's grinning like she's never seen a nightclub before and it's *amazing* and looks *exactly* like in the movies. I smile at her, and when she looks up at my proud and bushy face, she flinches and says, "Ew."

"That's right, baby, wanna dance?"

She scuttles off, making sure I can see how offended she is.

Moving past the vapid chattering children, I end up in the back room. It's dark, and Pit Mix is slumped in the corner while the rest of the team mingles and vaguely dances about. By the time I get to Pit Mix, the whole room looks fake, cheap, and flimsy, like some half-assed television stage.

"Pitty, this place sucks," I say, noticing his glass of champagne. *Nice. Pitty got class.*

Pit Mix lolls his head in my direction and slurs, "You don't pay for the sex, mate. You pay for them to leave afterward."

"I don't pay for shit!" I yell back.

His eyebrows go up thoughtfully, then drop back to their usual confused position. "Hey," he says, "where you been, man? We've been here forever."

"Dude, you like it here?"

"Well, yeah, why not?" He gestures vaguely at the crowd, which is not as dense back here as in the front room.

Target, Sadie, Cripple, and Jin are in the middle of the floor, all of them holding champagne glasses, except for Jin, who's holding an expensive-looking bourbon on the rocks. They look just as dissolute as everyone else, and it angers me. Now the club looks like so much paint on glass, nothing but a frail façade. I visualize a small rally car doing a ninety-degree slide through a blast of quartz and snow. The walls dissolve as the car spins through the crowd, mashing bodies, sliding on blood. Headlights twirl through a blizzard of glass and screaming faces. The ceiling shatters before it can fully collapse, and the sound is like ecstasy, electric rain sticks in a church, and then Pit Mix interrupts my thoughts.

"Hey, your Dead Assassin shit was really cool, man. How do you move like that? You're like a lizard, man." He changes hands with his champagne glass, and wipes the free one on his large stomach. Pit Mix is our lead driver, remember. Not our lead jogger.

"Thanks, man."

"You're gonna have to do your Wall Scorpion thirty times. You know that, right?"

"Yeah, so?"

"I'm just saying." Pit Mix looks down and absently touches a fur coat that's folded up on a couch.

"I have two Wall Scorpions," I say.

He thinks about it while fingering the coat. Then he looks up. "That's . . . sixty—"

"I know!" My chest tightens, even though this is not new information. "Dude, it sucks in here! This music makes me want to eat a dildo."

"What?"

Fake Oasis is ending fast, and I don't want to know what's next. "I gotta go, dude! If they play a fucking 'Smells Like Teen Spirit' remix, I'm going to punch you in the stomach."

Pit Mix considers this, but before he can say anything, "Smells Like Teen Spirit" pops on with a Teletubbies backbeat, causing Pit Mix to scream, *"You called it, dude!"* so I turn around and march out of the room without a word, clap my hands once and stride through the crowded main room with the coeds and the arcade games.

Time is a river, clogged with garbage.

I emerge into the warm night on Tchoupitoulas Street, where there's so much wet air and grapefruit blossom smell that I just can't help but smile, *really* smile, feeling the freedom for the first time all night. All month, maybe.

I decide to ankle it for a while.

I head up Tchoupitoulas toward Canal Street and do the usual people watching. Twenty or thirty minutes will do. It's Friday night, and the moon is nowhere to be seen. The rain has likewise taken a hike, so I'm going to hold my breath and dream the rest of the weekend off, drink lots of coffee and take naps and rehab Wolfblood and maybe read a *Dark Tower* book, or something comforting. And I'll definitely hit the gym and jack off a lot and maybe get a new tattoo. I'd like to find the seismographic readout from the Northridge Earthquake of ninety-four and get it wrapped around my throat. That would be a good use of the weekend. It can radiate from either side of my throat cobra, and the peaks of the seismograph can fade into a mountain range that crumbles down the back of my neck and avalanches into the mouth of the severed pig's head that's on my shoulder blade.

Fresh start on Monday.

Showtime, baby. It's time to make history with Pit Mix, and Ed Fury, and the One-Wheel boys.

Monday, baby.

Monday . . .

Monday, that's a long way away.

Canal Street appears, but the French Quarter is full of anxiety and aggression. When the smell of stale booze and vomit overtakes the rain, I change course and head over to the river where I sit in silence and smoke cigarettes while watching the barges and riverboats drift by. I wonder when I'm going to get drunk again, and if I'm going to kill myself before then. It's a good thing I don't have any guns in my hotel room.

I only have one emotion. It's unclear what it is, but I always feel like I'm a balloon drifting over a cactus garden. I'm cautious. That's why I'm covered in piecemeal tattoos. That's why people get out of my way. They know I'm breakable.

This makes me think about Ed Fury. How opposite a man can be, and how strange our energy is when put together. Fury has been clawing his way to the top from nothing, while I spend every day trying to destroy myself. Now we're meeting in the middle. Fury is afraid of me, but he doesn't know it. He's the Emperor, and I'm the impervious thief. I don't pay him taxes.

But despite his imperial demeanor, Fury is always grinning, and he's always shouting "absolutely!" and "fuck yeah!" Still, when he sees me, his face darkens, fighter's brow dropping over his eyes like a caveman. I know Fury grew up as some kind of underdog, inadequate in a mostly white suburb. He was never taken seriously. Just a tall Asian kid with bad skin who took karate and wore glasses, and he still thinks he has something to prove. He conceals his burden like a loaded gun. I grew up as a white boy in Los Angeles and went to a private school. I struggled in school, and I didn't do well. But my point is, Ed Fury grew up in Arkansas, and likely went to a district school, which means he was called a "chink" probably every day of his childhood. So, Fury has a different approach to fighting and wrecking shit than I do. He dug a cave beneath his mind hotel, a dark and cloistered dwelling full of lightless monsters. It's why he has that giant angel tattoo, the golden figure ascending his back, straddling flames, gliding upward through crescents of exaggerated musculature, brandishing a sword. The angel is clearly a symbol of duty, of rebirth and righteousness.

I have a thunderbird on my collar. Symbol of protection. The ragged scar on my chest stops in the thunderbird's talons, as if the tattoo actually protected my heart from that firetruck that tried to kill me.

But I'll admit, above the thunderbird is an angry cobra, floating up the front of my throat, jaws wide, ready to strike. There is calm in me—a quiet sanctuary, large as a lake. But there is rage in me as well—an occasional chemical spill—and if I'm not satisfied with one, I'll indulge the other.

In stunts, we have what's called a "1X." This refers to the number on the call sheet that identifies the main actor's stunt double. In *Everyone's Frankenstein*, Ben Schilling is number one on the call sheet, and Leon is 1X because he doubles him.

Darkness is my 1X.

It's inside me, coiled up like a cobra, ready to do all the hard shit, while my *real* self does nothing more than act.

179

Aurora texts me from my apartment in Harlem, forcing an all-too familiar pang of failure in my ribs. Do I languish after her? Maybe a little, but it pales among my usual regrets, nothing more than a distant breeze I can't feel under all my layers. My heart died years ago and has since been Frankenstein-ed together into some hideously low functionality. Or maybe I'm already married to the monkey on my back. She's asking about Wolfblood.

How's the chicken? she writes.

She's good! She's been lying on her back.

That's good?

Yes, Aurora, that's good. And she smells like rain again.

That's also good?

Jesus, Aurora doesn't know anything about cats.

Yes. That's very good.

I'm scratching Bloody's butt when it occurs to me that I could actually make it work with Aurora. Something brotherly assures me of this. Maybe I'll try again one day.

There's a chemical reaction happening in my hotel room. Underneath it, the plastery smell of bones boiling. The Gorgon's stare. The fear of night hours shrinking into nothing like a napkin on fire.

ROLLING, ROLLING

WE'RE SWEATING, AND we haven't taken a shit in three days. We consider picking up some crack, because that would make us shit bananas into a manhole. But most of the night is behind us already. No one is on the street but wandering drunks, mostly alone. Soon the light will arrive and ruin everything, and the roofers will reappear, tarring the tops of houses, and the shops will open, and the women will have lots of energy. But for now, New Orleans is in remission. We're having heat flashes in the dark, thinking furiously about nothing. Our legs are all herky-jerky, and we'd actually prefer nightmares to being awake.

We start filming in four hours.

Halona Jones has her flight booked for the following week, and we're both excited, although at this hour it only adds to our towering sense of dread.

A full moon rises over the courtyard at 2 a.m. It's large and dented, the color of tarnished silver.

Wolfblood is back to her full bloody self. Right now, she's perched on top of the towel shelf in the bathroom, making J's with her tail as we turn off all the lights, plug in our headphones, put on *The Dark Tower III* audiobook, and force ourselves to sleep.

Picture's up tomorrow.

Whatever happens, happens.

The morning is as pale and hot and loud as a goth chick with an infected septum ring screaming into a thousand microphones.

I arrive at basecamp a half hour early, and when I see Ed Fury, he smiles wide like a prince and says, "What's up, buddy!"

We bump fists.

"What's up, bro," I say, feeling optimistic because they gave me a 7 a.m. call time (much better than the dreaded 5 a.m.) and fully awake because of the Adderall I stirred into my coffee earlier.

"Hey Fury, can I talk to you for a sec?"

"Sure, bud!"

"I have some notes from the rehearsals with Schilling."

"Um . . . notes?"

"Yeah, like a list of ideas that Schilling had about his scenes."

"You wrote down a list?" Fury is worried, perhaps even scared. His grin falls off his face and shatters in the dirt.

"Yeah," I say. "Of ideas. From Ben Schilling."

Fury doesn't reply.

"You told me I'm not allowed to talk to Morley," I say, steeling myself. "Or Patricia."

He still doesn't speak. His eyelids twitch uncontrollably, an Asian supervillain ready with laser-eyes.

"I didn't write the list during rehearsal," I say. "I just did it last night, so I wouldn't forget the good stuff."

"OK," he says, recognizing the position he's put himself in. "What is it?"

"Well," I breathe. "In Frankenstein's Lair, the *finale* . . . He was thinking, like, there's this long fight, and then Frankenstein has a monologue that doesn't have any choreography, and it kind of kills the energy."

Fury is nodding his head in agreement.

"Schilling was thinking, why not keep the action going *while* he delivers the monologue? Keep the energy up, you know?"

Fury is nodding more excitedly now. "Mm hmm, mm hmm."

"So, Schilling thought it would be cool if during his speech, and this is if we have the budget—"

"The budget?!"

"Yeah," I say. "The budget. He can't do anything without paying for it, he knows that."

Fury crosses his arms over pectoral muscles that are the size of bulldogs.

"Ed," I say. I used to call him Ed before we were tight. "Schilling wants an injured SWAT guy to shoot him in face with a shotgun in the middle of his monologue. He says it might be funny if—"

"Lex!" Fury shouts.

"Yes?"

He takes a deep breath, then lowers his voice. "What's the name of this fucking film?"

"*Everyone's Frankenstein,* sir."

"No," he says. "That's not the name of this fucking film. The name of this film is *Universal Pictures' Everyone's Frankenstein.*" He glares at me. "Read the fine print, bro. Because you are the fine print. You work for the man. Not the movie."

This reminds me of the first day I worked on *Everyone's Frankenstein,* before I came to New Orleans. It was just a Covid test at Universal's high tower in Manhattan. I rode my Harley into the parking structure where a vast and utterly dystopian testing facility had been set up. The ceiling was low and sprawling, and there was barely any air.

As I dismounted my bike and walked toward the check-in, a slow procession of cars exited the structure. The faces inside them were crying, some sobbing, barely looking where they were going. It looked like a funeral procession.

They had all had Covid. And they had been denied entry into the movie. It's all fun and games until you realize where you are.

Time is a river, and it's fucking cold.

I say, "Yes, sir."

I wonder if I should tell Ben Schilling about this, about how it turns out he's not in a creative space, and the only people who are allowed to have ideas are Morley and Fury, and Schilling is just a puppet with a fancy name. He wouldn't take that well.

When Fury ends the conversation, he doesn't walk away like a normal person would. He just stands where he is with his feet planted and turns into a statue, looking past me.

"Alright, Ed. I'll see you later."

Fury holds up a fist, still standing like a slab, not looking at me. I bop it with my own fist and walk away.

Zelda's hanging costume pieces in my trailer.

"Zelda," I say, standing at the foot of the steps. "Can we fuck real quick before all this happens?"

She looks down at me. "No, Lex. Definitely not."

It's crazy that her tattoos always emit the same vibrance, no matter what the mood of the day is.

"OK," I say.

"Are you feeling alright?" she asks. "You look kind of . . . crumpled."

"Yeah, I'm fine," I say, giving her space to leave my trailer. "I just had bad dreams last night."

"You sure?"

"Yeah, positive. Unless you call being stuck in a tree while it crushes you a 'good dream.'"

"No," she says, "that doesn't sound good."

"What is that!" I say, pointing into my trailer.

Zelda looks over her shoulder. "What is what?"

"Those aren't the shoes I tried on."

She turns back to face me, amazingly calm for the first day of filming. "Right," she says. "So, we decided to go with a more tactical look."

"I hate them. They're too small."

"Lex, if you haven't tried them on, how do you know they're—"

"I can tell by looking at them. They're too small."

She sighs. "Do you want me to get your other boots?"

"No Zelda, it's fine. I'll wear them."

"You sure?"

"Yes. It's fine."

"Do you need anything else?"

"No thank you. I'm all good."

"Alright," she says. "Have fun, I'll see you out there."

"Hey, Zelda?" I call after her. She turns around. "Can you bring the other boots to set, just in case?"

She doesn't try to conceal her eyeroll.

"*Picture's up!*"

"*Picture!*"

"*Last looks!*"

"*Picture's up!*"

The AD is yelling for more atmosphere as everyone busies themselves like ants under an impending storm.

I'm rehearsing a "suplex," kind of a backwards pile-driver, which is really only a little bit cool, unless you're a monster that bursts into a bloody explosion when it hits the ground, which is Jason.

He and I are practicing our fight during the camera setup. Jason was hired as an ND (a nondescript stunt player), along with ten other ND's, creating the illusion of a large SWAT team, and a harem of hideous female monstrosities. ND stunt players are hired outside of the core team, either for hard gags—getting hit by cars—or easy gags like standing around holding a fire extinguisher off camera.

The fight Jason and I are rehearsing feels pretty good. But when I see Fury's expression, he already hates what I'm doing. He looks like he hasn't slept and wants to throw a tantrum. Fury walks stiffly over to us and says, "Do you want me throw a scenic pad down for you?"

"Yes, please," I say.

"I was talking to Jason." The pressure of Fury's hatred pushes me, then finally releases as he walks away shaking his head, and I'm stunned, not by Fury's overt rudeness, nor by the fact that he would withhold a scenic pad from me, but because Ed Fury—two hundred and fifty pounds of ambition—just made a joke, something I've never witnessed, nor even thought possible.

I'm smiling stupidly as a grip walks up to me. A gangly, crooked-looking trickster in a blue trucker cap, and he says, "Jeez, that guy's really riding your ass." Then he scratches his own ass, work gloves flopping against his thigh and adds, "He's watching you, brother."

"I know," I say, "I'm just trying to deal with it." I remember the gallon of CBD that I drank before coming to set.

"Hey," he says, leaning in, "you want me to sneak up behind him and turn off his walkie?"

I laugh. "Oh, my god, yes."

My instinct is to ask him where to get drugs, but I have enough already, and I'm not using drugs anymore, so instead I say, "Hey, I'm Lex."

"I know who you are," he says.

"How do you know that? This is the first day on set."

"I seen you around the stages," he says. He puts out a leathery hand and says, "I'm Red. People call me that because the color of my neck."

I laugh again, which twinges my back. "Nice to meet you, Red."

He smiles impishly. I like this guy.

The AD bellows, "Let's roll cameras!"

"Rolling, rolling!"

"Quiet all around!"

"We are rolling!"

The first six hours of the day are spent getting wide shots and establishing the fight. SWAT team versus monsters. We'll do the inserts and the wire gags throughout the rest of the week.

After lunch, we tackle the driving sequence. SWAT guys slide up to the Carondelet location in black Escalades and storm the place.

Since I'm not allowed to drive, it's shotgun with Pit Mix. We both have HK416 automatic rifles in our laps, ballistic helmets strapped to our heads, and shooting glasses on our faces. We can barely see. We're also not wearing our seatbelts because of the encumbrance of our thigh rigs, utility belts and lightweight armor plates laden with reload mags, radios, handcuff holders, knives, and sidearms. Also, because we don't really care about seatbelts.

All we have to do is squeal the car down Carondelet at thirty miles per hour and then spin into the entrance of Frankenstein's lair, along with four other Escalades. Pit Mix is the first in line, and the others follow. On a second bellowing "action" cue we'll leap out of the cars and file up the stairs, just like we did in the previz.

Through the windshield, colored smoke and white haze waltz through the intersection, as enormous crane lights and diffusers dangle over the street like nodding aliens.

When Pit Mix and I are in our starting position a block away, we hear the AD on the walkie say, "We are rolling!" followed by a chorus of faraway PA's yelling, "Rolling, rolling!"

I'm rocking back and forth, checking my rifle, and going over the action in my mind. Pit Mix shifts the car into low gear and turns to me. "Dude," he says. "Do you *really* think we landed on the moon?"

"What?"

"It's so fake," he says. "Have you seen that old moon landing footage recently?"

"Um." I'm thinking about the moon landing, and how fake the old footage actually looks. But then I think, *if film can be doctored to look real . . . then it can twice as easily be doctored to look fake, right? By conspiracy theorists and—*

"ACTION!"

Pit Mix floors it, and I can't help but grin as we accelerate toward the intersection. Screeching past the camera, he throws a one hundred eighty-degree spin and stops on our mark in a cyclone of steam. We pop out of the Escalade, and we all file in efficiently, charging up the stairs like medieval warriors, then spreading out across the upper balconies, aiming everywhere, searching for signs of The Creature.

"Cut!"

"Cutting!"

"Cut-cut!"

That went great! I tell myself.

Jin Hoon stomps over to me and says, "Dude, you gotta flank your buddies. You're aiming all over the place. Like this." He mocks me, aiming an imaginary rifle all over the place like a goofball.

"That looks retarded," I say, interrupting him.

"Yeah, it looks fucking stupid, dude. You gotta flank your buddies." He swings out an arm and pats me on the shoulder, hard.

"Reset!"

"Back to one!"

"Resetting!"

I gotta flank my buddies! I tell myself. *Of course. What was I even doing?*

I jog back down the stairs and climb into Pit Mix's Escalade, mentally measuring out how slowly I'll have to move up the stairs in order to flank my buddies and still look cool. Slow is smooth, smooth is fast. Also, flanking the camera looks really cool. I shouldn't doubt myself. I'm a fucking beast, and that's what they're really seeing.

Pit Mix and I drive slowly back to one, where we wait for the smoke and cameras and everything to reset.

Pit Mix explains to me why the moon landing isn't real. "Look at this video," he says. "It's so fake. Plus, why haven't we been back there since?" While I'm looking at the video, he adds, "People are saying Stanley Kubrick shot this when he was making *2001.*"

"Not possible," I say. "Kubrick's shit looks way more real than that."

"Well?" he says. "That's what I'm saying!"

"But don't we have specimens?" I say, reasonably. "From like, moonrocks and—"

"ACTION!"

Pit Mix floors it again. We slide through the intersection in a swirl of atmosphere, leap out of the SUV like fleas from a dog, charge up the stairs, and spread out. And I flank all my buddies, as the Steadicam leads us artfully backwards, and Frankenstein explodes through the doorway, stepping into the debris, raising up his lightning gun, and pulling the trigger.

"Cut!"

"Cutting!"
"Cut-cut!"

After five takes we get the shot, and at last I have a break.

Red, the grip and I go out by the two-bangers (the bathrooms) to smoke a cigarette. He's telling me about the time a federal agent confiscated two pounds of weed from his grip truck when Ed Fury walks by. Fury sees us smoking and stops dead in his tracks. The look of horror on his face buckles his usual self-awareness, and for a second he appears helpless. He turns to look behind himself, making sure none of the higher-ups are nearby. In a trembling voice, he utters one enormous word.

"Smoking?"

I just look at him.

Fury finds his footing, rights himself and says, "You're smoking, bro? You're gonna . . . That's gonna kill you!"

It's Red who speaks up. "Hey, my grandfather's one hundred and three years old!"

"And he smokes!?"

"No," Red says. "But he minds his own fucking business."

Fury points a finger at me, forearm bulging. "You don't smoke on my set," he says. "Throw that shit away." His finger curls back into his fist, and before he finishes climbing the steps into the two-banger to take a shit that's obviously overdue, he turns back to me and adds, "And go to the gym, you fat baggy fuck."

It doesn't make any sense. Ed Fury's the guy who called me in the first place (while I was peacefully asleep in my bed, I might remind you). He's the one who offered me the contract. And now he's furious! I think he hates me, even though I've already done this much for him. Rehearsals with Ben Schilling are going great, and the movie is looking hopeful. It's going to be sleek and well-rehearsed. What is he thinking? Making me feel like I'm pulling him down? Trying to pull me down first? I'll blow this whole place up! I'll topple the walls and hit the fucking red button! Fuck Ed Fury. You want to antagonize me? You want to start shit by calling me a baggy fuck? Making me feel like a washout in front of Red? Get in the ring, motherfucker! I'll stomp your imperial ass, you bloated, humorless fuck!

THE STUNTED MAN

FALL DOWN ONCE, GET UP TWICE

THE YEAR IS 2694, and the first day of filming finally ends.

Now it's the second day, and we're all in the upstairs hallway. A hilarious new gag is in front of us. According to Fury, a SWAT guy is going to face off with Frankenstein on the second-floor landing. A Mexican standoff, or whatever. But before they can draw down, Frankenstein shoots the floor with his lightning gun, causing the heavy floorboard to Teeter-Totter and launch the SWAT guy into the ceiling. Then Frankenstein blazes through a few more guys, and at the end of it all, in a corridor of smoke, he turns to face the camera. The area behind him is clear. There's a beat, and then the guy that was Teeter-Tottered drops from the ceiling with a hard *splat*, comically timed.

"Mike and the guys finished rigging the Teeter-Totter gag last night," Fury says. "It took a fuck load of overtime, but they got it. Whoever wants it can have it."

Uncomfortable silence. *No, you go first.*

Jin Hoon shrugs and says, "I'm forty-six. I ain't doing it."

Another long pause, so I say, "Yeah, I'm forty-six, too."

Jin doesn't glance at me, nor seem to hear me at all. Why does he always do this?

I've noticed Jin's reticence toward the group lately. It's not just me. Most of the time, he's barely here at all. Perhaps Jin is using the same psychological tactic as me. To us, at our age, stunts is becoming a memory, so we start to look past it. This way, when we finally quit the biz, we won't miss it too much. Just like lovers at the end of their run, there's a distance. Still, Jin's caustic negligence makes him come off as superior, like he's checked out all the time.

I mumble, so no one can hear me, "Forty-seven in October."

Target takes the Teeter-Totter gag, of course.

Meanwhile, at the Wollcroft Hotel there have been fire alarms. All the time, from 7 a.m. Screeching, high ceiling nightmares, and I haven't slept or napped, and Wolfblood's been in my suitcase for three days, looking like Garfield in a giant lasagna pan.

On Friday, the finale in Frankenstein's lair is meant to be completed. But there is still a ton of stuff that hasn't been shot, so we know it will be a long day. Friday's a day shoot, but since we're indoors we can go as late as we want because on Monday we're switching to nights. Everyone will get their fifty-six-hour turnaround, as per SAG rules, regardless of what time we wrap.

Rushing to set, already behind schedule because my costume was wet when I showed up at 5 a.m. and I insisted that Zelda dry it for me, I take an Adderall, hoping it will make the day more pleasant while the rest of the crew freaks out about everything.

Friday starts with a oner. The stuntwomen who play Frankenstein's bride hopefuls who escaped the "playroom" and dropped to the first floor like cockroaches are now fighting the SWAT guys, and losing. Despite their incredible strength, they're disadvantaged by numbers and weapons. But when Frankenstein descends the stairs, hosing away three guys at once with his lightning gun, he joins the fight, easily destroying what's left of the SWAT team.

A "oner" is basically the same as a "long take." The Steadicam operator is now part of the choreography, flowing through the scene while multiple actions happen around him. Bodies launch, practical effects detonate, windows break, all in one continuous shot, causing the audience to feel as if everything is happening around them, and also causing the actors to show real exhaustion that makes them look more human, and turn out a generally more heroic performance. It takes a lot of rehearsal to nail a oner that's as large in scale as this one. Er.

The first action in the shot is the three ratchet pulls. Cripple, Pit Mix, and I are blasted by the lightning gun, flailing through the air on invisible wires, heralding the arrival of

Frankenstein on the first floor. From there, the camera follows Frank as he tosses his gun aside and fights through six more tactical guys. After that, he checks on a few dead bride hopefuls (showcasing the gruesome makeup effects of the undead), and at last terminates what's left of the injured SWAT team. The shot ends with Frankenstein stomping the final SWAT dude's head—an animatronic dummy—shattering his helmet and crushing the brain within.

If at any point during the take someone messes up, we reset and start over. This means that Cripple, Pit Mix, and I have to do our ratchet pull as many times as it takes to get the whole shot. We have one thing to our advantage, however. Cripple is going through a glass window. Pit Mix and I are going into the wall, but Cripple can only do his gag as many times as we have breakaway windows.

When I ask Damon, head of special effects how many breakaway windows we have, he says eleven.

"Eleven!?"

"Yup." He scratches his face lazily. "Morley wants this shot to be everything."

"Well," I say hurriedly, "how many head-squashing dummies do we have?"

"That's makeup effects," he says. "But I think they have four."

"Four!?" This means we can start the shot eleven times and get to the end four times. "Jesus Christ," I say.

"Yeah," Damon agrees. "Jesus is gonna have to look the other way on this one."

Four days of tactical bullshit have rendered my feet with blisters, and my boots are killing me as I sprint from the transpo van to the bank entrance on Carondelet, late because my costume was wet. Mike the head rigger stops me in the doorway and orders me to grab two four-inchers and a tombstone from the rigging truck.

"I have to check in with Fury first," I say, panting.

"No," Mike says. "Safety first. Grab the pads." So, I spin around and jog across the street to the truck.

By the time I get inside the bank location, everyone is rehearsing and chattering like angry donkeys. The noise is dizzying, hitting my face like unwanted air. I slip my Covid mask off for a second. No stress, I'm Red Zone.

"Lex!" someone shouts. I don't know who said my name because I'm holding two giant four-inchers over my head, and I can't see very much around me.

Jin Hoon appears very close to me and shouts, "Throw those pads in the room behind that window." He's pointing somewhere. "Those are for Cripple. Then come back here for rehearsal."

"I have to grab one more tombstone."

"Leave it," he says. "I'll have Sadie do it."

Someone else shouts, "Grab two!" and I think it's Cripple, but I've never actually heard Cripple shout.

"What about my props?" I say. By this I mean my helmet, flak jacket, utility belt, firearm, and various Velcro patches.

"We'll prop you up later, shit! Let's go!"

I bring the four-inchers into the room where Cripple is landing.

Rehearsal is unimportant for me. Since my action is first, and we're not rehearsing on wires, I just throw my hands in the air and yell, "doosh!" right after I hear, "action."

The Adderall kicks in.

I'm simultaneously aware of everything, yet unable to triangulate who's saying what. Everyone's wearing Covid masks, so I can't see any mouths moving. All the voices blend together with equal urgency, which causes a low anxiety to crawl under my harness like spiders.

The window that Cripple is going through looks good. It's not breakaway glass, but tempered glass with small explosive charges taped to it. Damon from special effects will detonate the glass in the moment Cripple hits it, creating a more exciting effect.

Beneath the tempered glass window is a second, smaller window, with an air conditioner built into it. This window looks like regular, "annealing" glass, which is dangerous. I check Cripple's leads, and they look pretty good. He's going to be on two wires, attaching to his harness at one pick point. This will launch him up and back, I'm guessing thirty psi with a seven-foot stroke, no deceleration, forcing him to arc freely through the window where an eight-incher, two four-inchers, and a couple of ND stunt guys holding tombstones will catch him.

After thirty minutes of confused and petulant rehearsal, we are ready to go. The prop guys pile twenty pounds of crap on me, as the riggers clip me into my wires. The circus is about to begin.

In the first take, after Cripple crashes through the window, Ben Schilling forgets his choreography, and we go again.

It takes fifteen minutes to clean up and reset the glass, as the art department adds more fake blood to the floor, and everyone goes back to one.

In the second take, the camera guy trips on someone's hand halfway through the fight. From video village, Ed Fury is heard yelling, "Guys, remember your death!"

We reset.

In the third take, Ben Schilling forgets his choreography again. I secretly remind him to drop his hips, assuring him that "slow is smooth, smooth is fast. They can speed it up in post."

After the seventh take, I unclip my wires and sneak outside to vape some nicotine during the reset. Red is out there, and he hands me a cigarette. An elderly woman walks by and says, "Hey, what y'all filming?"

Red replies, "Mister Potato Pants Six. Revenge of the Horny Cauliflowers."

The woman sneaks a glance through the doorway and yells, "Alright, y'all! Be safe in there!" and walks away.

On the eighth take, Cripple goes down.

There's too much fake blood on the floor. When Morley calls action, Cripple is yanked backwards, but his feet slip. The wires cast him head-first into the air conditioner that's set in the lower window. The real glass shatters at the same time the tempered glass above him explodes, burying Cripple in a pile of glass, unconscious.

Everyone screams, "Cut!"

"Cutting!"

Ed Fury rushes over. Nobody else moves. For once, the enormous bank location is silent.

Fury shouts, "Where's the fucking medic!"

Cripple is soaked with blood. But it's not clear whether it's all fake, or if some of it is real. The shattered glass is equally undiscernible. If Cripple is bleeding, we have no idea where. He looks like an earthquake victim.

An overweight, young-looking dude strolls up wearing flip-flops and slowly pulls on a pair of blue nitrile gloves, looking down at Cripple with no expression on his face. He says, "Sorry, I was outside. What happened to him?"

Horror happened. That's what. The big fucking what-if.

It takes almost ten minutes for the ambulance to arrive. I'm smoking out front on the street while Sadie and Target complain that there was never an ambulance ready on set. Cripple is wheeled away on a stretcher, still unconscious. Jin rides with him to the hospital.

Orange wheels, not blue.

We don't set up for another shot. Ed Fury orders us all back to basecamp for a department meeting. A one-hour hold before lunch, paid for by Universal's high-risk insurance.

It's 11:30 a.m. and the stunt team stands in a circle outside their trailers, some shifting on their feet expectantly, others slumped in forfeit with their arms crossed.

"Guys, I can't believe this happened," Fury says.

I'm not pleased by the warble in his voice, nor the odd color in his face. He looks like his wife just divorced him with full custody. I prefer the other Fury. I can't hate this one. I realize I'll never be his friend. I'd prefer to scoff at Fury's arrogance and put myself above him than watch him actually struggle.

Fury continues. "We all understand the risks involved. There's always something random or stupid that can be over-looked."

"Is Cripple OK?" Sadie says.

Fury closes his eyes. "Yes. He's good so far," he says. "He's awake, and he's not badly hurt. He has cuts on his hands and face, and he might need stitches. They're still do-ing tests on him, but so far, he's OK." Fury looks up at the sky as if he forgot it was there. "I can't believe there was no ambulance on set," he says. "That's my bad. It'll never hap-pen again. I've already talked with Patricia about it."

Target says, "Yo, that medic was an idiot."

"We already got a new medic," Fury says. "That guy was a fucking idiot."

Everyone nods.

"Now, listen. Do you guys want to go home and take the rest of the day off? It's OK if you do. We lose the loca-tion after today, but we can pick up the rest of the fight at the stages with green screen."

There's a pause, and we all look at each other.

"If we stay here, we can finish the fight without Cripple. We'll do a camera wipe after Cripple's wreck, and it'll still look like a oner—kind of."

Another pause, until finally Sadie says, "I'm good for another take. Let's do this for Cripple."

We all agree. Target says, "We'll get it in one, sir. Let's fucking do this."

And Leon adds, "Fall down once, get up twice."

Stunt people have the stupidest sayings. That's supposed to be inspiring? All this positivity is nothing more than passive-aggressive cajoling. Jocular intimidation. In fact, with me it's the opposite. When I fall down, it's twice. Once my body falls, and once my spirit. But only one of them gets back up.

Everyone agrees with Leon's idiotic slogan, and Fury says, "Lex, Pit Mix, do you remember how you died?"

Neither of us respond.

"I told you to remember your death."

I say, "I don't remember how I died."

"Me either," says Pit Mix.

Fury sighs. "It's OK," he says. "We have it on camera. We can figure it out. Good job, guys."

We continue working until 10:30 that night. We get the oner, also some inserts and star moments with Ben Schilling, then the Teeter-Totter gag with Target on the second floor. It's a long day.

The first week is over. The blisters on my feet will heal. The shoulder I separated on the sixth ratchet pull will probably heal. The finale is in the can.

And Halona is coming soon. That's one thing I'm sure of.

THE STUNTED MAN

FALL FROM HELL

ONE WONDERING THOUGHT, however, pollutes the day.

Women love it when you ask them questions. They're compelled to give answers. But when I ask Halona Jones if she likes oysters, I'm perturbed by her silence.

In fact, I haven't heard from Halona in four days—almost a week. Because of this, it's impossible to get out of bed on Saturday morning. Also, because Wolfblood, who has finally rejuvenated to her full ragtag self, is sitting on my beard, resting her head in my mustache, and purring loudly.

Dinner last night was Cheez-Its, followed by some soy sauce that I sucked out of the packets at some point in the night.

Hunger eventually draws me out of bed, and as I walk into Butcher on Tchoupitoulas for a muffuletta sandwich, I have no idea that a hole is about to open beneath my feet, swallowing the path, and everything on it.

Sobriety is human, but getting drunk is divine.

The muffuletta lands with a cappuccino and a side of warm breezes rolling off the Mississippi from the east. The afternoon sunlight illuminates everything. There are no shadows here. No secrets. Everything is clear.

My feet are severely blistered from those boots. They were too small. Even with two missing toes, I knew it. I told Zelda. Also, my shoulder has a sharp pain and limited range of motion, and one of my ribs is badly bruised from when I wrecked against the second-floor balcony.

Under normal circumstances, I can't see beneath what's ailing me. My anxiety is physical, and my inner feelings just relate to whatever my body senses. On a day like today, I expect to feel defeated and remissive, but also generally confident that after two days of rest and a week of rehearsals with Ben Schilling I'll be OK. I have no reason to doubt my resilience. Today I live. Today is a new generation. Butcher's illuminated patio and the muffuletta sandwich say exactly that. But after I pay my check and waddle to the bathroom, tiptoeing as if I have glass in my shoes, all these warm thoughts evaporate.

It's a private bathroom, the inside plastered with stickers and graffiti. A Barbaric Fury sticker has been crookedly adhered to the hand dryer. After buckling my jeans and grabbing my leather vest off the hook on the door, I turn to flush the toilet.

What I see erases everything.

A small constellation of cocaine sits on the back lid of the toilet.

Primal instinct kicks in, as I pull out my driver's license and gather the tiny crystals into a clump. I lick my index fingertip, stick it into the small pile and plunge it into my mouth.

The first thing I feel is confusion. Then my heart starts to punch. The stress only lasts a few seconds before I wash my hands, say thanks to the bartender, and lurch out onto sunlit Tchoupitoulas. I duck into the liquor store on St. Joseph, snatch up a six pack of IPA's and a six pack of lagers, walk through the Wollcroft corridors to my room, hurl myself into the bathroom, snatch up the Excedrin bottle, open the bag of coke, dump it onto the sink, get startled by Wolfblood, pick her up and put her out of the bathroom, close the door, cut and sculpt all the coke into four lines, blast through two of them, rub my nose, then push my face so it's three inches away from the bathroom mirror and stare at myself.

Yes.

The Beatles' song "Something" drifts pleasantly around my head, slow motion and mellifluous.

Houston, we're back online.

I can't let Bloody into the bathroom. She loves this stuff more than I do. In fact, as I open the door I have to push her with my foot before slamming it shut. Bloody's body is now hard, like a stubborn bowling ball.

I grab an IPA from the bag, put the rest of the beers in the fridge, and go back into the bathroom to take another shit. Coke does this to me; I can set my watch by it.

I hoover another rail on my way out.

Staving Wolfblood with my foot again while trying not to fall over, I see my phone is lit up and vibrating.

"Hey, Fury, what's up?"

"What's up, buddy!"

"Nothing's up. What's going on?"

"Oh, not much. Good job last week, bro!"

"Um, same to you."

"Yeah, bro," he says. "So, rehearsals with Schilling next week . . ."

"Yeah?"

"You good for it? Do you have all the previzes?"

"Yes, of course."

"OK, sweet. Leon's doing OK?"

"Leon's great," I say. "Talented son of a bitch. We're all getting along great."

"Dope," he says. "That's what I hear. So, just a heads up. You're going to have Behind the Scenes photographers and documentary people in rehearsal with you next week."

"Sweet," I say. "Double contract."

"No," he says, annoyed. "You owe Universal all that shit. Promotional material. It's in your contract."

"Damn."

"Yeah, so listen. I'm gonna need you to style your beard, and like, clean up the stunt gym a little bit."

"Um . . ."

"And don't wear that Cannibal Corpse T-shirt."

I wish I could stand up, but I'm already standing, so I go back into the bathroom and say, "I'm not touching my beard unless I get a double contract."

"Excuse me?"

"I'll brush it. And I'll put some conditioner in it, but I'm not trimming it."

"You'll need to trim it next week for the Dead Assassin," he says.

"I'll breach that castle when I arrive at it."

"Dude!"

"I'll look good, Ed, don't worry. Hey, how's Cripple doing?"

"Lex, do *not* wear that Cannibal Corpse shirt."

"What the hell!" I shout. "Universal loves corpses! They built their whole empire on fake corpses. And—"

"It's not Universal," he says. "It's like a sponsorship, televised thing."

"A sponsorship?" I scoff. "Let me guess, Nike and Puma are fine? You got a preference here? Fury's personal aesthetic, not mine? You got a sponsorship?"

"Lex—"

"Look," I cut him off. "I'm an independent, dude. This is me they're seeing. I'm making *you* look good in all this. And Ben Schilling is more metal than all of us! A schilling is literally a piece of metal! He's gonna wear his leather pants, and Leon's gonna do all the Adidas placements or whatever, and I'm gonna march up my own fucking mountain the way I always have." Small pause, during which I snort half of the fourth rail. "Fine!" I say. "I won't wear my Cannibal Corpse T-shirt!"

There's an uncomfortable silence, and I realize that I might be on speaker phone with the producers.

"Hello?"

"Dude," he says. "My kids are here. I gotta go."

"But I might wear my Tragedy T-shirt."

Fury sighs. "Is that a band?"

"That's a great band."

"OK, whatever."

"Hey, how's Cripple doing?"

"Lex, please just remember that you're on camera. It's a fucking show, dude."

"I'm always on camera!" I shout. "And I always look good! You want to tell me I don't?"

Fury's tone plummets. "What the fuck did you just say?"

I have no idea what I just said, so I say, "Look, Fury, I got this. The three of us are going to do great. We'll be the new face of Hollywood. In startling 8K, HD, whatever. Don't worry."

There's a pause, and Ed Fury clicks off the line.

Noticing myself holding a cellphone in the bathroom mirror I say, "What the fuck just happened?"

I text Leon. *You got any weed, dude?*

He replies a minute later, which feels like an hour. *Of course, bro!*

Where did you get it?

Unfortunately, marijuana's illegal in Louisiana because God loves the South. But Leon has the skinny. After a few texts, I know exactly what to do.

Lots of people are at the swimming pool, including me. But I'm not interested in swimming. Instead, I'm pacing around uncomfortably, looking for a black guy named Vick who works at the hotel. Leon texted me his photo, and I know who he is. I've seen him around. He's some kind of janitor or something.

It isn't long before I see Vick wheeling a trashcan across the courtyard. The sun is starting to go down.

I walk up to him, smile knowingly, and say, "Hey man, you want a cigarette?"

"Yeah, son, no doubt," he says. "What room you in?"

"Six-two-six."

"Yeah, son, no doubt. Give me five minutes."

Forty-five minutes later, Vick knocks on my door. I buy an eighth of weed off him. It looks good, so I ask if he knows where I can get some blow.

"Yeah son, I got you," he says. "Give me ten minutes."

An hour and forty-five minutes later, The Howling Wolf Tavern is a galvanized hive of energy. It's also the closest and shittiest bar to the Wollcroft.

A small room at the end of the bar has death metal blasting from it, and a man sits by the door with a stack of bracelets, typing on his phone. Sweet fucking deal.

To the left, past the bar and the bathrooms there's a much bigger room.

I order a glass of whiskey and a Juicifer, then move to check out the bigger room.

A fat bouncer guards the entrance, wearing all black. He's turned the other way, talking to some ladies, so I slink past him into the room unnoticed, emerging into a huge, interactive burlesque theater piece. The girls are acting crazy, and the crowd is going nuts. Mardi Gras beads are everywhere, and bras and panties hang from the ceiling like cobwebs in a haunted house. The lighting effects are all yellow, purple, and green, swirling over everyone. Smells of weed, sweat, and booze create a haze thick enough to float on, while men and women stagger everywhere, wearing feathers and holding cocktails in glowing lightbulbs, large plastic souvenir cups, or highballs with LED lights in them. EDM music crashes into a thunderous marching band, becoming a fanfare that causes the lights to gather into a greenish white sphere on the stage. Small cardboard tractors roll onto the stage towing tiny Mardi Gras floats filled with women who jump out and begin their dance routine, peeling off layers, shucking themselves down to their pasties. Everyone is screaming.

It's a theatrical reenactment of Mardi Gras, complete with women flashing the stage while plastic landfill crap is chucked at their heads. One woman is bleeding. Another is topless but has so many beaded necklaces that her breasts are buried under their bounty.

After a couple of short acts, I decide to check out the smaller room instead. My feet are killing me, and perhaps there's a place to sit down in the death metal room. Also, I need another round of drinks. The energy in the big room has already reached a fever pitch, alarming me that the balconies are going to collapse, and I might be stuck in here forever.

Before leaving the room, I'm startled by two women who have trapped me between themselves. They must like my new neck tattoo. Northridge Quake baby, that's me. They're gyrating on my legs. One of them has on a tight green dress, the other a Cat in the Hat costume. There's a man behind the Cat in the Hat with his dick out, and he's dancing with his arms in the air as if his dick is nothing but a costume piece. All of this is fine with me, except my feet are scorched, and one of them is leaking a hot, sticky goo.

Excusing myself, my eyes pounce onto a young girl dressed as an alley cat who looks exactly like Wolfblood, which causes me to scream and charge for the door.

"Double Sazerac and a Faubourg, please."

"Whoa, dude, you feeling OK?"

"I don't give a shit!" I say. "Double Sazerac, and *two* Faubourgs, please."

"I can only serve you two drinks at a time, brother."

"*Triple* Sazerac, and a Faubourg, you fuck!"

"Hey, you alright over there?" A man at the end of the bar is pointing a can of PBR at me. He's wearing wraparound sunglasses and a grey shirt with an American flag printed on it. I imagine the back of his shirt says something like "STOMP MY FLAG, AND I'LL STOMP YOUR ASS."

"I will be," I tell him, scratching my beard as if I'm clawing my mask off. "I'm trying to get into that death metal room. Only it's not death metal, it's downbeat raw punk with hardcore influence and a bit of thrash—*fuck!* The whole world is falling apart!"

I turn back to the bartender and wait impatiently until my drinks are served. Time is a river, brimming with melted flesh and eternal screams.

The man at the end of the bar is still watching me, and I don't like it.

"What's the deal, man?" I say, but he only shakes his head and continues to watch me through his sunglasses.

After slamming half my Sazerac I stand up, wincing at my feet, and take the two drinks into the bathroom to do bumps of cocaine off my switchblade. When I return for another drink, Stomp-My-Flag is still watching me from the end of the bar. I'm gonna give him two minutes. Two minutes, and after that I'm going over there to give him something to stare at me about.

Two minutes go by, and I'm about to get up and go over to him when *he* gets up and comes over to *me,* saying, "Hey buddy, what's up. Let's go outside."

"What's outside," I chuff.

He glances at a nearby table with four or five men sitting at it and says, "Fresh air. Let's go smoke some weed or something. Come on."

We leave The Howling Wolf, turn right, and wrap around the corner of the building. St. Joseph turns onto Tchoupitoulas, where it's dark and mostly quiet. A large Prevost tour bus is parked at the sidewalk, creating a small alleyway between itself and the building, out of view from the street. As we step into the narrow space, a light rain begins to fall.

I remember saying something like, "Shit, I need my jacket," and then someone behind me shouts, "Hey, fat boy!" and I hear a loud *bink!* as the back of my head explodes.

Flashing red and blue lights rouse me slowly to consciousness. This is followed by an off-balance vibration in my head, which forces me to roll over and vomit onto the sidewalk.

"I think he's just drunk," someone says.

"Yeah. Looks that way," another agrees.

"Hey, man, we're gonna get you up to sitting. Hang on." Grabbing hands, and I'm propped against a wall, sitting cross-legged between two empty picnic tables.

I manage to garble, "Bloody . . ."

"Yeah, you scratched your face pretty bad when you fell. But you're OK."

"No," I say. *"Bloody."*

"Stand clear, folks," a cop says.

One of the men who assumed I was drunk turns to the cop and asks, "Can you guys take him home?"

"Yeah, no." The cop puts his hands on his hips, then sticks his pelvis out. "We can't do that."

"Well, what can you do?"

"We can either take him to the hospital or leave him here."

"Oh," the guy says. "Well, can you get his wallet out of his pocket? See where he lives?"

"Ha! No." The cop is standing over me, chewing on a coffee stirrer and grimacing, as if I were a dead hooker in the middle of his daughter's birthday party. "We can't do that either."

The ground is wet, and a slight but steady rain falls. I know from the way I'm sitting that my wallet is nowhere around. Likewise, my coke and switchblade. I'm not upset about the wallet, but the knife is an insult and a tragedy. It was a wrap gift after three seasons of *Locke & Key,* a five hundred dollar, double-action Infidel, the name "Mercier" engraved on its hilt.

"Sir," the cop says to me. "Do you want us to call you an ambulance?"

I shake my head, looking down at my lap.

"What was that?" he bellows.

My fists clench. "No, sir," I say. "Thank you."

"Lex!" a woman shouts. "Is that you?"

Very slowly turning my head, Luisa and Shredder appear at the corner of the building. Shredder is tugging at his leash, wagging his tail, trying mightily to reach me.

Luisa helps me to standing, while the cop watches us.

"Jesus, the back of your head is bleeding," she says.

"Yeah, I fell pretty hard."

I'm leaned against one of the picnic tables. A small crowd has gathered outside The Howling Wolf. Costumed freaks in Mardi Gras masks mingle with punks, some of them wearing mohawks, two belts, and metal spikes, the other ones more modern—scowling, threadbare college dropouts with fists instead of hands.

Stomp-My-Flag is nowhere around.

I mutter, "Fuck."

Luisa turns to the cops, who are smirking, apparently satisfied that I, a vagrant metalhead, got my ass kicked. "We live right there," she says, pointing. "I'll take him home."

Luisa and Shredder help me back to my room. The night receptionist gasps when she sees me. We explain to her that I'm OK. My hood is up over my head, burying the bloody gash that's dripping all the way down my back into the waistband of my jeans.

As we approach my door, Shredder starts whining, barks once.

"It stinks in your hallway," Luisa says.

"Does it? I didn't notice."

"Can I come in? Help clean you up?"

"No," I say. "Thank you. I have a first aid kit in my stunt bag. I also have peroxide, for Bloody. I'll be OK." Shredder is sniffing at the crack under my door.

"How *is* Bloody?" she asks.

"She's good," I say. "She's perfect. Listen," I sway quietly for a moment. "You can hear her purring through the door."

"I don't hear her," Luisa says. "Wait, maybe." Then she shrugs. She leans me gently against the wall and stares hard into my eyes. "You have a concussion," she says. "Don't go to sleep."

"I won't," I say. "Thanks, Luisa." I look down. "Thanks, Shredder baby." I ruffle his fur, which doesn't seem to comfort him. He's still sniffing at the door.

"Alright," she says. "Fall down once, get up twice." She pokes me in the stomach. "Call me if you need anything, alright?"

"I will, thank you. Hey, Luisa, don't tell anyone about this."

She glances at my door and frowns. "Yeah. Sure," she says. Then to Shredder, "Come on, boy."

Shredder runs down the hallway, away from my room. Before they round the corner, Luisa looks back at me uncertainly. Then she's gone.

My mind hotel is a bombed-out, flame-riddled war zone. Shrieking ghosts of memories and old hotel guests swirl through the rubble like smoke.

I enter my room and pick up Wolfblood, stick my face in her fur, and breathe in deeply.

Then I text Leon. *Dude, I've been in a fight.*

When he texts me back, I'm already on my second IPA, which is actually my tenth, or thirteenth drink of the night. He writes back, *Sweet, dude! Did you send it?*

I swallow hard. *No. I was robbed.*

Stripping off my leather vest and tossing it onto the floor, I notice the bathroom door and freeze. My mouth goes completely dry.

The door is open.

I kick off my wet boots and hustle toward the bathroom. There had been a tiny line of bingo dust that I'd left on the basin. Now there isn't.

Wolfblood leaps onto the sink, arrogant to show me what she accomplished while I was out, and proceeds to lick the basin some more, purring as loud as a motorcycle with an open choke.

My phone buzzes, a new text from Leon.

Yanking Bloody off the sink and tossing her onto the floor, I somehow get my phone in one hand and a towel to wipe off the sink in the other. Then I push Bloody with my foot and scream, "Bloody, you *fiend!*"

Leon's text message says, *Fuck, dude. Do you need anything?*

Catching my breath, I check my reflection in the mirror. The scrape on the front of my face is starting to bruise.

I write to Leon, *No, thanks. I have everything I need.*

Then I text Halona.

We need a physical therapist! Help! Can't wait for you to get here!! [emoji]

She doesn't reply. It's after midnight, so she's probably asleep.

THE STUNTED MAN

RAGING VOID

FOR AN INSTANT I dared to shake off my chains and look around myself with a free and lofty spirit. But the iron had eaten into my flesh, so I sank again, trembling, and hopeless, back into my miserable self.

Halona's not coming.

This feels like a certainty. I haven't heard from her since I booked her flight last Monday, and I recognize the behavior. But now, all of a sudden, her absence feels like an obstacle, something I must break through.

Five weeks left on the old Frankenstein Express. After this week of rehearsals with Schilling, we have two weeks of Swamp Fight, one week of Hospital Fight, and the last week will be the epic battle of the Farmer's Cottage: Wall Scorpions, oil and fire, and lots of ND stunt players.

We awake on Sunday with a raging headache. The hotel room is blurry. After trying to examine the blood that's spattered all over our pillows but being unable to focus our eyes, we decide to take ourselves to a hospital.

The gash on my cheek is only superficial, and the swelling of my face is considered to be a "good sign." But the wound on the back of my head is serious, and in need of staples.

Now there's a nasty bald spot on the back of my head where ten hideous black staples crawl over my skull like ants.

The doctor warns me to stay away from bright lights for at least a week. Also, no heavy lifting, and no swimming. When I tell him about my plan to spend two weeks in a swamp surrounded by explosions, the doctor laughs and says, "Well, *that* should be fine."

When I get back to my room, I call the boss.

"What's up, buddy?" Fury says.

"Um, Ed. I have a problem."

"Oh yeah?"

"Yeah. My face is fucked up. Like, more than usual."

Fury sighs and says, "What happened."

"I was mugged last night. Pretty bad. It wasn't my f—"

"Send me a picture."

I send Fury a picture of my face, and one of the back of my head.

"Dammit, Lex! Why can't you stay out of trouble?"

"It wasn't my fault," I say. "These guys jumped me."

"They just jumped you? Unprovoked?"

"Yes. I was right by the hotel. Look—"

"Did you fight back?"

"Um . . . yeah," I say. "I leg-kicked one dude so hard he spun around, and then I punched him in the face, and he dropped. Then I threw another guy on the ground. After that they—they got me." I'm only embellishing to protect my reputation.

"Lex," Fury says. "The PR department is coming to your rehearsal tomorrow."

"Yeah. I don't think that's a good idea. You should call them off."

"Call them off!?"

"I can't be on camera like this, Ed. It'll look ridiculous."

There's some shuffling on his end. "You're putting me in a very difficult situation, Lex."

"I know," I say. "I'm sorry."

"We're shooting the Swamp Fight in one week! How are you going to wear prosthetics if you don't have a face! The makeup department's gonna freak out!"

"Well, I *have* a face. It's just . . . rearranged a little."

"It's gonna get infected in the swamp. This is a fucking mess."

"It's not a big deal, man. I'll wear bandages. A water-proof wig cap. Fall down once, get up twice, right?"

"You're never working for me again," he says.

"I already know that."

There's a very uncomfortable silence which I end by saying, "Look, Ed, I got this. I'm already dialed in. The Swamp Fight is gonna be great."

"I gotta go, Lex. I'm hanging up now."

"Call off the PR guys."

"Obviously!"

"You can bring them in on Thursday. The swelling will be down by—"

"No dude. You're not showing up on my set with a gash on your face. You realize how that will make me look."

"Yes, sir."

"I'd tell you to get your shit together, but I don't believe that's even possible."

"It wasn't my fault!" I shout, but Ed Fury has already hung up. "And yeah, I'm fine, by the way! No major brain damage or anything, you . . . you . . ." But I can't find the words. My brain is too swollen. No room for language.

The sun goes down in a slow, bloody haze. Just like my career.

Halona never shows. Her sweet, nymphlike image fades into the dark distance, along with all the others.

Fury puts me on hold for the week. Leon agrees to be Ben Schilling's movement coach, and the BTS photographers, documenters and PR team all show up to perform their fabulous promotional circus.

Monday morning, I find Miss Jenny at the front desk. When she sees me, she covers her face and squeaks, "Good Lord."

"Hey, Miss Jenny. I've been in a fight."

"Are you all right?" she says. "What happened?"

"Look, I got blood on my bed. I was wondering if I can get some new sheets."

She types a few keys on her computer, looks up at me and says, "Mr. Mercier, you haven't had your room cleaned in weeks! Why don't I arrange for our cleaning staff to come in later today?"

"No thank you," I say, "I brought my own cleaning supplies." Or maybe I said, "I *bought* my own cleaning supplies." Either way she seems dubious, so I add, "The room is in good condition. I'm kind of a stickler."

"Well, alright," she says. "I'll have someone bring you a new set of bedclothes."

"Thank you, Miss Jenny. I'll leave the dirty ones outside the door."

"That's fine," she says. "Man, you look *messed* up."

"Please." I hold up a hand. "Let your staff know that there will be blood all over the sheets."

Miss Jenny gives me two large garbage bags to put my sheets in.

On the way back to my room, Leon glides past me on his One-Wheel, skids to a stop and yells, "Bro, what the fuck!"

I explain to him that I won't be in rehearsals this week. Leon asks if he can use my minivan, to which I oblige. I don't have my driver's license anyways. After handing him the keys he says, "Alright bro, I'll hit you up. Be safe. Don't eat any more asphalt."

I smile, showing my jagged front teeth and say, "Don't usurp my position as movement specialist."

Leon throws his head back and cries, "Usurp!" then glides away silently along the carpeted hallway, and out of sight.

And the week goes by in a flash flood of responsible drinking and minor drug use. A lot of exploring the city, and not much staring out the window. I remain hidden the first few days. My face is so swollen, my body so racked with pain that even friends feel like a weight on my back. But on Thursday I call the boys, and they agree that it's time to cause some serious trouble.

I make an effort to look good. Lots of hair conditioner, chancy suit clothes, sunglasses. Something about injuries makes people look homeless. Perhaps I overcompensated, because now I look like a professional wrestler's nemesis, but hey, it's almost the weekend, and someone has to look good around here.

Thursday night is really great. Until it isn't. After only a few hours of drinking, the ambulance comes for us.

We're at Harrah's Casino, and I'm talking with Target and a guy named Galway who was hired to do some fancy driving. This week they're filming a car chase while Leon rehearses the Swamp Fight with Ben Schilling at the stages.

We're seated in barstools around a tall table in the corner of Harrah's. Leon's off somewhere playing poker, while Pit Mix, Sadie, and Luisa haunt the bar. Jin is sitting with the three of us, typing expressionlessly on his phone.

Galway's an eager beaver. Young, blonde, and un-marred. He was born into the stunt industry and bred for driving. Galway talks a lot, especially to me. He's telling me about a recent gig in Oklahoma, all the gnarly shit he had to do on camera, and the prankish debaucheries in the hotel. He's wearing a shirt that says, "GRAVITY IS NOT CON-SENSUAL," which I love, even though I have no idea what it means.

All my senses are on fire. I'm trying to understand the complicated wallpaper while simultaneously evading Galway's constant questions. He must be a fan of my work. Then all at once, without any warning, the fire goes out. Cold fumes consume me, and before I can steady myself, the whole casino rolls upside down, and the floor swings upwards into my face. Our table, carrying a tray of oysters and four martini glasses crashes on top of me soundlessly, and I'm asleep.

Thirty minutes later, Sadie and Luisa walk me back into the casino to get my jacket. The rest of the team is slumped nervously at the bar, until Target sees us and shouts, "It's *alive!*"

"What happened?" Leon asks.

"The paramedics ran tests on him," Sadie says. "He's dehydrated."

"Oh," they all say, nodding. "That makes sense."

It's amazing to me that no matter what, no one will ever believe their friend is using drugs. Even when all the signs are there. It's a mental block. All seven of them (including Jin and Leon who have actually *seen* my drugs with their own eyes) believe that I was dehydrated. Suspicion is a rare and fleeting muse. It requires a lot of details. And I've been there too; stared a friend right in the eye as he told me he had allergies, while anyone who didn't love him would've assumed he was on heroin. It's some kind of anomalous, subjective blind spot, and it's always there.

Thank God for that.

When the dull ambience fades and the team is more or less themselves again (Pit Mix holding back his humor while Target makes all the jokes), I excuse myself to go home.

"But you haven't finished your water," Sadie says.

"It's OK," I say. "I'm gonna drink some Gatorade at the hotel. Anyways, this place is fucking donkey."

"Why do you always have to insult a place before you leave?" Sadie says.

"Yeah, we like it here," adds Luisa.

For a moment, I just stare at them through my sunglasses. Then I say, "I'm sorry, guys. I'm just . . ."

Doomed . . . Damned . . . Damaged . . .

"I'm just dehydrated," I say. "Later, fucks."

"Bro, it's only nine-thirty!" Target protests.

"I shouldn't be here," I say. "I don't gamble, and I don't take selfies. I have no business being in a casino."

"But—"

"I'm out, guys!" I stuff my hand into one of my pockets and give Target a hundred-dollar bill. "That's for the oysters and martinis. Sorry about that."

"No way, dude. Keep it."

"Don't argue," I say. "I'm leaving. Hail Satan."

I can feel them watching me as I leave the casino.

I don't return to the Wollcroft, of course. Like my man Target said, it's early. And Graveyard Rodeo is playing The Dungeon tonight. So, I head there instead for a relaxing, much needed sound bath.

The show is good, but I only last long enough to hear a couple of songs. The flashing stage lights and glaring reflections off the band's cymbals and metal hurts my eyes, causing a loud whine in my head that doesn't match the key they're playing in. Remembering the warnings from the doctor about my concussion, I decide to head back to the Wollcroft after all. Because I'm responsible. And I need to hydrate and ice my face before the Swamp Fight on Monday.

Outside The Dungeon I don't feel drunk, although I am stumbling and unable to see above ground level. The sidewalk is paved with crushed oyster shells and cement. A homeless man walks past me and says, "Man, I'm so hungry!" I give him five bucks. Another homeless man walks past me and says, "Man, I'm so thirsty!" Noticing the water bottle that's in my hand, I stop walking and say, "Hey!"

The homeless man turns around. He's very short and looks exactly like Charles Manson, dirty, with an air of unmitigating evil. I show him the water bottle, and he holds out his hands. Carefully, I toss it to him, but it falls between his outstretched arms and explodes at his feet. I shrug, turn around and continue walking back to the hotel.

New Orleans, mon amour, I'll see you tomorrow.

Friday morning, Leon tells me that Ben Schilling isn't in the mood to rehearse, so I can have the van if I need it.

The car guys are off today, too. Apparently, they slayed the driving sequence without incident.

I'm heading to Rouses Supermarket for some groceries when I find Target, Pit Mix, and Galway stumbling around the parking structure, singing "Sweet Child o' Mine" at the top of their lungs.

"Y'all want some *crack?*" I yell from the van as I roll by. They're on the passenger side of the van, so I lower that window to let out my witticism. They start cheering, "Lex!" and they open the passenger door and crawl in altogether, dumping themselves into a pile next to me. Target lies down across the dashboard, mostly obscuring the windshield. Thinking this is some kind of joke, I continue driving slowly down the ramp and out onto St. Joseph Street.

Pit Mix shouts, "We're going to Barcadia!"

Galway roars in agreement.

"It's nine-thirty in the morning," I say. "They're not open."

"They're open," Pit Mix says. "I checked."

"That's definitely not true."

"Barcadia!" Galway screams.

Target is asleep on the dashboard.

"Guys, I'm going to the supermarket."

"We're going to Barcadia!" Galway screams again.

I pull over to the curb. "Hey Target," I say. "I can't drive like this. Come on, dude." I poke him.

Target rolls off the dashboard and worms his way through the open passenger window, dropping onto the sidewalk, unconscious.

"Um. Guys?" I say.

They laugh and take pictures of Target until Pit Mix says, "I'll help him! I'll bring him back to his room."

"How are you gonna do that, Pitty? You're way smaller than Target."

"Not where it counts!"

"Dude," I take a deep breath, which hurts my rib and shoulder. "He's dead weight. You'll never—"

"I'll help him too!" Galway shouts. He and Pit Mix exit the van, and I speed off without looking back.

In the Rouses parking lot, which is sunny and surprisingly cool, I get a fresh idea. Without thinking too much about it, I pull out my phone to text Aurora.

Hey girl! Wanna come to New Orleans? Bring Jake?

She doesn't respond right away.

Pit Mix sends me a video while I'm halfway through the grocery store. I pull over to the side of the beer aisle and watch it. He and Galway are dragging Target by his feet, face down, through the lobby of the Wollcroft Hotel. Target looks like a grotesque Superman, flying backwards along the floor. Other guests look on in confusion at what appears to be a corpse being stolen for parts. Miss Jenny is frozen in rapture, and in fear.

Better him than me, I think.

That's a long hallway.

THE STUNTED MAN

SWAMP FIGHT

MONDAY MORNING I wake up sometime in the Triassic Era, so I can be at work by 5 a.m.

Four weeks left on the old Frankenstein Airlines Flight 626.

Aurora is coming to visit me in three weeks, after the Hospital Fight—sans Jake. Why would she do that, you ask? It's unclear. Maybe because she's been my friend for eighteen years and wants to hang out in New Orleans. Or *maybe* because she wants to dump Jake and move to California with me forever. I can't wait to ask her.

My face is a throbbing warzone. The back of my head, no better. My right orbital is definitely fractured. I never had it X-rayed, but my eye socket feels like it's packed with shattered glass, and it buzzes like a forgotten guitar amplifier. My rib, however, is only bruised. I'm pretty hopeful about that.

Sadie gave me some ointment for my bruises. When I went to her hotel room to pick it up, I became aware of just how far I'd drifted from myself. Sadie's room was full of energy and wellness. Massage guns, foam rollers, healing ointments, and crystals were placed everywhere. A tiny yoga studio had been built into the corner where tennis balls, yoga blocks, and an electric muscle stimulator had been neatly arranged. Books about health and anatomy and chakras were stacked on her desk, and the room smelled of lemon oil, and inner peace. And of course, I felt nervous, as though I might burst into flames from the wholeness of it all.

Back at my apartment in Harlem, another cat has died of relay toxicosis, possibly from ingesting a poisoned rat. But here in the Bayou, a dark silence surrounds New Orleans like the primordial fringes of the universe. I haven't been to set yet, but basecamp is already beautiful and sprawling, a cluster of movie trailers canopied by trees that sway pleasantly in the mist.

Because the Dead Assassin is billed as a "scripted character," I don't have to do any other part in this scene, unless they give me a double contract. My only obligation is a fight with Ben Schilling and Leon, along with various establishing shots and whatnot. This will only take four or five days, even with digital scanning. The rest of the two weeks are all mine. If I'm not in the shot-list noted on the call sheet, they might not even call me in. But I am called in today. And although the call sheet is vague, I know I'll be in makeup, and I'm pretty sure I'm going in the water.

Said makeup application takes three hours, with two highly invasive artists. They jab my face and paint me down with medical adhesive. "Telesis," it's called, and it's moderately toxic, and highly flammable, and they're using hard, prickly paintbrushes instead of makeup brushes which hurts, especially around my cheekbone and eye socket. It's freezing in the makeup FX trailer, so after David Bowie's greatest hits plays on repeat for three hours, I'm relieved to step outside into the hot air.

"Holy shit!" Sadie cries as she walks past me.

"Pretty rad, right?"

"Dude, you look terrifying! Like, if Leatherface and Skeletor had a *love child!*"

My face is made up of three faces sewn coarsely together. My right eye and left ear are open mouths, frozen in a soundless scream. My hair is a greasy mess of cholesterol and Spanish Moss.

"Wait until they put my contact lenses in," I say. "It's fucking sexy."

Sadie's bouncing on her toes, so I add, "You look good too. Who did your makeup?"

"Janelle," she says. "I wish she gave me open eyes, like you. I can't see a damn thing."

"Other than how good I look."

"Anyone can see that!" She laughs, but her frightening mask barely moves. Sadie's eye sockets are also mouths, but they're stretched into agonizing sneers. Her whole face is a grimace of strain.

"Hey," I say. "Cripple's back. He's playing The Creature's bride hopeful."

"Yeah, I saw that on the call sheet," she says. "I hear he's wearing a woman's fat suit."

"That's hilarious. I can't wait to brain him, and then chuck him into the swamp."

"Her," she corrects. "Brain her."

"Um, them? This feels like a them situation."

"Yeah, maybe."

"Hey Sadie," I say, "when Leon smashes me at the end of the fight, do you think I should wear a back pad, or a chest pad? The action is confusing."

Sadie considers this, a monster clutching a Gatorade Zero. After a moment she says, "You should quit stunts."

"Hey, Lex!"

I duck. Cammy, the basecamp PA, is rushing toward me between the trailers. "They need you on set. We're flying you in. Oh god, you look fucking terrifying!"

"Thanks, Cammy."

"How about me?" Sadie says.

Cammy throws her hands up and says, "You guys are both scary as fuck."

"No, I mean, am I called to set too?"

Cammy fingers her walkie and says, "Oh yeah. They're asking for all stunts on set. Let's get you two in a van."

The day is spent moving from island to island, as we capture different setups and establishing shots all over the swamp. Frankenstein roams around with his bride hopeful while the scientists hide out in one of their laboratory house boats, and their creatures wander the swamps. Eventually, the creatures pick up Frankenstein's scent and shamble in, rustling in the bushes until, in a sprawling bog thick with atmosphere and stippled shadows, Frankenstein faces off with the horde of undead. The imagery is surreal. There's a psychedelic music to it.

Frank tells his enormously grotesque girlfriend to hide behind a Black Locust tree. Cripple gives the performance of his life.

But before the beatdown ensues, the Dead Assassin appears! He's humorless and hungry, wearing, you guessed it, a cape. Frankenstein spins around to face the Dead Assassin, only to find his bride hopeful cowering before him. The Dead Assassin snatches the hopeful's head and smashes her face into the tree, killing her, then tosses her into the swamp like a bag of rotten crawfish.

Then I say my first line:

"Dear Alpha, you have no need for such wasted experimentations. Although you are noble, your work is futile." I glance at the corpse in the water as it bobs and gurgles, then look back to The Creature. "Come with us. Let us study you. And we shall fashion you a bride, the likes of which you could never imagine. Through her, you will come to accept the nature of your being. She will bring you what you seek. And she will love you."

That's one of my two lines.

Frankenstein snarls at me. The snarl becomes a thunderous roar.

I do my cape flip.

David Morley screams his approval, and the rest of the crew applauds with him. The smoky haze is crawling sideways, which catches my cape and floats it for about two seconds. Everyone is delighted by this, despite the obvious knowledge that it's August, and coming up on hurricane season.

After all this is in the can, we still have five setups that remain to be shot. It's not yet four o'clock, but rather than continue, we're forced to break for lightning.

The next three hours are spent in a people mover, taking cover from rain and lightning, begging the transpo driver for air conditioning.

Hunched in the back of the bus I pull out my book, *Stay Out of New Orleans*. But after a few pages I have to put it down because it feels good to be out of the city. A light but stinging rain covers the marshland, and it's beautiful, a sprawling mosaic of great oaks, cypress, water hickory and slash pines. To be clear of the chaos and trash and scary porch dwellers is refreshing. I've seen enough beer bottles and broken strands of beads and Styrofoam takeout containers and prostitutes littering the sidewalks, weed-choked asphalt riddled with black scabs and potholes like the street itself has STDs, and that blue dog follows me everywhere, smelling like rotten oysters, so I don't need to read about all that right now. But, it's the only book I brought to set, and it's still a good conversation piece, so I ignore the rainy quiet of the marsh-lands and continue reading about corpses buried beneath kitchen floors in the French Quarter, mutilated slaves, and marching bands that are actually rapists, flooding my mind hotel in a deluge of urban pre-Katrina horror. Because why not? We love this stuff. If we could eat the garbage and hookers and stabbings without getting sick, well, we proba-bly would.

At 7:30 p.m. we go back out to the swamp for another couple of shots, but we don't get them because there's an-other lightning strike three miles away, so we wrap for the day.

It seems casual enough because it is. Casual is my game. We show up, do our bit, slam Cripple's face into the tree, have an iced coffee, don't think about the toxic prosthetic glue that's sucking my face into a disturbing expression that's not my own, keep the Advil and Adderall coming, sign out exhausted, make noncommittal agreements with the boys, take a Xanax if I'm going out to dinner, drink a couple of beers by myself to prepare for the next day, which is always suspicious, raid the medicine cabinet, cry into Wolfblood's fur, pass out, play it serious, watch out for snakes in the swamp. Not just for me, but for my friends, too. I'm under a spell. I'm casual. I buy a twelve pack of Yuengling lagers and give it to Miss Jenny at the front desk with a wink and say, "This is for you and your staff," and she blushes, and it's all perfectly casual.

Not a lot of snakes on set; just one sighting so far. Our "swamp" is actually in the bayou right next to a massive swamp. It was dug out with heavy construction and filled with treated water that production recycles every three days. The floor of the swamp is quicksand that's lined with tarps weighed down with sandbags and concrete blocks. Better watch your step. But thankfully, there are no resident leeches or snakes or gators in our swamp. They all live next door. Still, it feels alien to dig an enormous hole in the bayou, fill it with water and spend seven days wading in it.

Next week: night shoots. A whole different set of animals.

But for now, I'm on hold for a week. According to the script, the Dead Assassin meets Frankenstein during the day, murders his undead companion, then slinks away as Frankenstein fights through the horde of creatures to get to the scientists who are hiding in one of the floating laboratories. The sun goes down as the brutality ramps up, and when the last scientist is killed the monsters swarm the laboratory and drag everything down into a watery Hell. Then, after a brief and chilling silence, the Dead Assassin reappears, vapid and expressionless, standing on the roof of the half-sunken houseboat, cape waving in the wind, the last light of sunset glinting in his eyes like fire.

The two creatures lock horns in a battle for undead survival. The Dead Assassin is bludgeoned, then mauled to death with a canoe until he's nothing more than smoking bubbles in the mire. A swirl of pink blood, coke-laced beer foam, and floating bits of gristle so much my remains.

But that's next week. For now, the rest of the crew is stuck wrecking in that faraway location while I'm getting wrecked in town, fuckin' all, walking and drinking, drinking and walking, indulging in the Big Easy nightlife while occupying myself with various nefarious substances.

I wonder what kind of wreck Target's doing tonight. I'm sure my imagination doesn't hold a candle to it. That dude can send it. Pit Mix doesn't have any idea what he's doing, but he can send it too—especially when he's driving. And don't get me started on Leon. It's a great team. Sadie's a walking explosion, take my money.

I try to pick up women throughout the week, but I only get lucky once. Her name is Lindsey. Or Rachel. One of those. We end up going to her place, so I guess she actually picked me up.

After the one, however, I'm not so lucky. Once my shattered face heals, I'm not as interesting anymore. Anyways, I'm not looking for sex. Far more important things are on my mind. Like music, and drugs, and squirming around beneath the surface of things.

I don't remember much from that week. Only vague, disordered visions of following one pair of pants to the next, alternating fragrances of azaleas and night blooming jasmine merging into rotten crawfish and sweat, the fusillade sounds of children drumming on buckets, ducking into music clubs where free-falling rhythms ricochet off pressed tin ceilings. I was a one-man marching band, until I took off one of my boots to snort cocaine off of and someone ran by and snatched the boot from my hands. Now I'm a three-hundred-pound skeleton, shimmying through the crowds, head weightless and off balance, feet unstoppable. Throngs of chaos in the Quarter. Police on horseback slipping on broken strands of beads while Jesus freaks with enormous crosses plead repentance into megaphones, getting soaked by Huge-Ass Beers. But I refuse to repent, smoking joints on the riverbank with skaters because I'm a one-man parade, and my Northridge Quake neck tattoo is turning heads, and if I stay out late enough something will happen.

I remember trying to get out of bed one morning but being unable. Instead, I'm spread-eagled on my mattress, vibrating uncomfortably, glitching like a video game character. My throat is hot and dry, and my sinuses are clogged with scabs making it difficult to breathe. The alarm on my phone is going off, which means I'm supposed to go to work, and when someone says, "Turn that thing off!" I realize it isn't my mattress I'm lying on. After calling Aurora and crying about how useless I've become, I check the call sheet and discover I'm not actually working today—I only set my alarm by accident.

Zelda and I go out to dinner one night, but it doesn't go well.

We're at Ruth's Chris Steakhouse of all places, and Zelda gets very drunk and whines the whole night. She tells me the same thing over and over, that she's been in New Orleans for three months and she ran out of Vyvanse, a very strong medication for a case of ADHD that borders on insanity and renders her autistic. She wants to go home to L.A. where she can reup, but she's afraid to ask her boss for a day off, and she's certain that everyone knows she's an addict. I assure her repeatedly that strong medications are totally normal these days, but she's too drunk to appreciate that. Instead, she just whines and cries, explaining to me that if she doesn't have Vyvanse she wants to scream all the time. Zelda's mind hotel is one of those "no tells" you see in the fringes, crouched beside highways, the kind with empty vending machines and fluorescent lights endlessly sputtering madness. I offer Zelda some Adderall, but she gives me a confused expression and declines. So, we go back to her place and smoke heroin for a few hours. In the morning, when the roofers show up silhouetted in the hazy sky, I head back to the Wollcroft for some rest. The jagged path beneath my feet has vanished.

The roof of the sunken boat laboratory is slippery and hard to fight on. Leon hits hard, but I can take it. I land him some good ones, too. I'm pissed off because my boots are slipping, and my back hurts. I could go to sleep in the spiders and chigger-infested undergrowth, I'm that over it.

But Ben Schilling gives me good energy. He's funny, and a joy to watch. I also like the way the crew chills out when an A-Lister is on set. They act all quiet, like nervous birds around a cat.

Zelda's following me around everywhere, asking me if I want a hit. But all I want is to get this done and drink the two Faubourg's that are in my trailer, and then maybe think about it. I have some coke at the hotel anyways.

On the third night, after thirty hours of swamp-fighting, the boat comes down and crushes me in a bloody, splashy mash, and I'm wrapped. The whole crew magnetizes toward me with hugs and applause while I stand with my hands on my knees, steadying myself. Fury shakes my hand, pats my shoulder, and walks away.

I'm rushed into a black sprinter van and delivered back to basecamp before I can say thank you to Leon or Ben Schilling. A massive Charlie horse inhabits my left thigh.

Slumped on the narrow couch in my trailer, exhausted, I listen to the rain falling outside. It sounds like footsteps creeping everywhere. A storm is coming, and I'm sitting in it, waiting for a chair to open up in the makeup trailer. When it does, I'll sit in that too. Don't care what time it is. I'm just glad to have my knees and elbow pads off. And my baseball sliders, best of all. There is no sweeter relief than taking your pads off after a fifteen-hour day.

There's a knock on my trailer door. Target opens it and steps inside to congratulate me.

"How's your body feeling, bro?" he asks. Target comes off as sincere, while at the same time within an inch of telling a joke.

I don't say anything. I'm thinking about double overtime.

"You fucking sent it today," he says. "I got a lot of it on video."

I don't move. Not even to adjust my sunglasses, which look ridiculous on my monster face. I widen my knees a little and say, "What's up, Target. How's the arms dealing industry?"

He makes a confused face, then says, "Well, dealing *and* manufacturing. See, Georgia state licensing incorporates—"

"Dude," I open my legs a little wider. It's hot in my trailer, but my knees and elbows are as free as Eskimos. "Let's go get a handle of Jack," I say. "And a twelve-pack of Faubourgs."

"Uh," he says. "Fuck yeah. Alright."

"Liquor store across from Mulate's. Then shower. Then your room. Tell everybody."

In the makeup trailer, I'm rubbing shaving cream all over my hands and wrists while Matty removes my wig with an alcohol spritzer.

Today was a fat motherfucker.

As Matty rips apart the back of my bald cap, my sweaty hair is released. It's cool and wonderful. He dips his paintbrush into the oily Super Solv, wetting it as drippy as possible, and starts removing the glue that's adhering the Dead Assassin's face to my own. As soon as my right ear breaks free, I feel the oxygen on it, and I can finally hear properly on that side, which causes me to tremble with pleasure.

My whole body relaxes, as I take in the reality that I'm done for the week. I become emotionally excited about my mask coming off. It's always freezing in the makeup FX trailer, but this time I like it. Matty paints and pulls and peels the prosthetics slowly across my face diagonally, while the oily Super Solv slides down my nose and chin. It pools in my eye sockets, and I'm almost crying with relief. When most of my face is off, Matty wipes my eyes and ears with a Kleenex, then steps away and comes back with a wet face towel. The shaving cream has dissolved into my hands, diffusing the makeup that's been reapplied two dozen times throughout the day, and I use the wet towel to wipe all the brown and green gunk off of them.

I take one of Matty's sponges without asking and dunk it into his container of Super Solv. Then I go to work on my hands and wrists and fingernails. Matty's doing the same thing to my neck. The sound of rain begins to pepper the roof of the trailer. Matty steps away, then comes back with a burning hot face towel. He hands it to me, and I wave it once in a cloud of lavender steam, place it over my face and say *"Aaaahhh!"*

The hot towel is then used to scrub the remaining makeup around my eyes and mouth and also my slimy hands. Behind the ears, the best part.

"Is that rubbing alcohol?" I ask, pointing to a small, un-labeled spritzer bottle.

"Yup."

"Can I use it?"

"Of course."

I spritz my hands and wrists profusely, then spray it once in my mouth. The green paint around my fingernails and in the creases won't relent. I rub them for a bit, adding Super Solv so my hands don't dry out, then scrub them with one of the old face towels.

Throwing the two towels into the trash I grab a Wet Wipe and get busy with the tiny beads of glue that are stuck on my neck and beard. Matty comes back with another burning hot towel, which I wave once, press to my face, and say, *"Aaaahhh!"*

I toss the final towel in the trash, apply some moisturizing EDAP on my face, stand up and thank Matty. I give him a hug, then walk to the other end of the makeup trailer to say goodbye to the other two artists who are doing a similar thing.

Then I step out into the bright, rainy morning.

Seven a.m.

I quickly put on dry clothes and collect my things from my trailer. Satisfied, I look for Cammy the basecamp PA to sign out.

Normally, we would gather at the front of basecamp to sign the G. But since it's raining, no one is outside, so I go to find the production trailer.

Cammy is sitting in the production trailer with the G (our timecard), squashed in by seven lumbering stuntmen and their bags. She's looking down despondently at the paperwork. The air is quiet.

"What's up," I say. "What's wrong?"

No one answers.

Leon clambers in with his enormous bag, taking up more space than he has.

"She says she has to sign us out at six," Target says. He folds his arms, then looks at Jin.

"This is so messed up," Sadie says.

"It's fucking bullshit's what it is," adds Pit Mix.

Jin sits in the far corner of the trailer, elbows on his knees, looking down.

Cammy looks up from the G. Pale and exhausted, she says, "I don't know what to do, guys. Production says I have to sign you out fifteen minutes after you wrap." She sighs and puts her hand on the walkie on her desk. "I can radio them again."

Luisa says, "Yeah, that's in the SAG agreement, but it's implied that when we're wearing prosthetics, we sign out *after* we get our makeup off."

Cammy's voice is weak. "That makes sense, but I don't know what to do about it."

Leon speaks up, and God bless him he isn't trying to be rude, but he's tired, and he doesn't read the room. He leans against the wall and says, "We're done whenever we're fucking done."

Cammy starts to cry.

I say, "Watch it, man. Be nice. We'll settle this."

Jin snaps his head from the floor to me, and for the first time he's impressed. A suggestive smile flickers in his eyes. I wonder if he actually never heard anything I've said before now.

Jin says, "I'll text Fury. He'll figure it out." He slowly shakes his head as if all the burden is on him, and begins typing on his phone. Outside, the rain falls in slashes, entombing us. Two minutes later, Jin sighs and says, "Cammy, just sign us out at seven. If there's a problem later, we'll deal with it."

Cammy nods, hair dangling over her desk in defeat.

We sign out, and the rain mostly clears. Another ten-minute storm.

"How're you doing?" I say to Leon in the parking lot.

"Hey, bro," he says. He's rubbing his eyes, squatting on his stunt bag in the mud. "Those prosthetics sucked."

"Yeah," I say. "Like having a plastic bag over your head, with spiders in it. But we did it, dude. That shit looked cool. I think we might have actually crushed it today."

Leon lifts his head and peers up at me from under his red cap. "It was fucking spectacular, bro." He holds out his fist. "Your cape flip at the beginning was epic. Target got a video of it."

"Killer," I say, scratching my hairline.

I bump his fist.

"Hey," I say, "I know a place we can get some cocaine and pay some college kids to try it for us to make sure it's not poison. Wanna go?"

Leon blinks at me in the bright, seven-thirty sunshine, and smiles. "Dude, one hundred percent," he says. "I gotta shower though."

That night, after a day-long party in Target's room, Leon and I hit The Little Easy. It's a small and rowdy dive bar on Julia Street, open all night.

"Let's get out of here!" I say to Leon, shouting over an invasive Four Non-Blondes remix. "This place is kinda, I don't know, donkey fucked."

"Sure," he says.

"Why do the hottest girls always go to the stupidest—" my throat clenches, and I freeze.

Across the bar, Ed Fury is leaning against a wall talking to some young boy who's looking down, grinning, shifting on his feet. Fury runs his hand through his hair, trying to be nonchalant. He's not acting like himself. Is Fury gay? I mean, he has a wife and kids, but this is some pretty gay-looking stuff right here. I have to get out of here before he sees me.

I clap my hands once. "Hey Leon! You got that bag?"

"Right here, bro."

I grab the coke and high-step it out of the bar, never looking back, emerging onto Julia Street in a daze. I start grabbing at my throat, trying to get it to relax. My other hand is clenching a planted magnolia tree, but I think it's a patio umbrella, until—

"Hey dude!"

I turn around slowly, vision returning down a long tunnel. Leon is standing next to me. So is a magnolia tree.

"What happened? Are you OK?"

I take a huge breath, which is a bad idea, then look up at the stars.

"It wasn't the Four Non-Blondes, was it?"

"Fury," I gasp. "Gay." The stars begin to canter, then fall. "I think he saw me."

Leon says a few things, starting with "what?" but I don't hear anything else. I'm looking at the stars so I can connect everything, but the sky and the buildings are spiraling horribly, and I'm torpedo-spinning through the blackness.

Now I know why Fury hates me.

He wants a piece.

Fuckin' A.

We end up on the river with a couple of Faubourg's in our hands, crouched beneath the shadow of a Marriott Hotel where no one can see us. The air smells like oysters and silt, the ground as soft as late-era Metallica. The brisk nostalgia of the river is lost on me, however. I am beyond humanism.

Slowly, a barge appears. It's as long as four city blocks, and about as high, lumbering down the river like an unanchored prison. I jump into the air and throw the horn sign, yanking at the air above me, not expecting anyone out there to see me. A second later the blast goes off, causing a tidal wave of sound that floods the city. Everyone in New Orleans wakes up and cowers, as I scream seven-fold under a winking, pill-shaped moon.

THE STUNTED MAN

WRAPPED

HOSPITAL FIGHT, BABY.

Except it's not a hospital fight anymore. It's been changed to a vet clinic fight. As per the latest script revisions, hospitals are too public for Frank's low-profile capers.

But oh boy, The Creature's secret veterinarian is actually a mole! The vet calls the authorities, and they whisper things like, "he's here" and "we got him."

Then the evil government scientists storm the place. They've brought with them a new monster, one that shoots fire out of its mouth. That's why we're all doing fire burns. This new monster is completely CG, but the fire is mostly practical. We have every license to destroy the building, since production has paid to have the vet clinic relocated to a bigger spot. All the pets and medicine have already been re-moved.

Two weeks left on the old Frankenstein Advent Calen-dar. After that I'll arrange to move back to California, start a new life and maybe quit stunts altogether. Eventually, we all have to pack up our youth and trade it in for something.

Could I actually marry Aurora and settle down? Commit us both to beer bellies and a wealth of memories? Aurora knows about my dark lapses, my wasted seasons in the abyss. But that's all behind me now. If I give up performing, I can give up hustling as well. Forget about the movies altogether. The circus, the death metal façade, everything. Go retire in a beach town. Answer the call. Ultimately achieve greatness as the world's sweetest, most beaten down bartender.

But all of that is future stuff. For now, we must destroy this vet clinic.

Fall down once, get up twice.

I have an ear infection from the swamp. I'm not going to tell anyone about it. Also, my eye socket is still fractured, and I still have staples in the back of my head.

The holding area is a narrow strip of Astroturf with a suffo-cating dog piss reek and a hot, Venusian atmosphere.

We're in the rear enclosure of the vet clinic, hugging a low stucco wall fenced in by chain link, sitting on folding chairs in an oval formation. Loud fans are blowing, but they're not helping the heat nor the stench. Hurricane season has receded for now, and a peculiar dryness hangs on the air, a premonitory welcome, or a warning of some kind.

Sadie is on her feet, practicing a three-person fight by herself, in the corner.

Pit Mix, Target, Jin, Luisa, and Cripple are seated in their chairs, hunched over their phones. No one knows what they're doing.

I'm doing an online questionnaire to see which circle of Hell I'm going to, according to Dante.

Leon is practicing some lazy tricks on his One-Wheel, headphones in as usual.

It's earlier than Layne Staley's death.

I rattle some Advil into my mouth to busy myself, and that's when the gate opens, and Ed Fury walks in.

"What's up *guuuyys* . . ." He scans the stunt holding area, rubbing his hands together greedily. "Welcome to second unit."

Fury has shaved his beard but forgotten his mustache. The sight of him, an Asian Hulk wearing tight pants and a tank top with a mustache and a walkie talkie, confuses everything.

The team offers an amazingly tired, "yay," and I wave a desultory coffee cup in the air.

"Lex," Fury says, pointing at me. "That cape flip last week? Fucking epic. That's the trailer right there."

"Hell yeah," I say, nodding.

I need to get laid.

After a brief pep-talk, and a short dissertation on fire safety, Fury brings us into the building to walk through our actions for the day. Thirty minutes have been allotted for rehearsal, because we haven't been to this location yet.

"Boom! Fire Monster crashes through that doorway. We'll put Pit Mix there, Cripple there, and Target there. Lex, we'll put you in that intersection, because you're gonna do your Wall Scorpion in *there.*" Fury points to a small room with windows in the side of the hallway. It used to be a show-room, where cats who were ready for adoption lived. One wall is glass, visible from the entryway. Another wall—*my* wall—has a giant purple kitten painted on it. It's grinning toothily, innocently, with a rainbow in its mouth. The room is decorated with cat trees, toys, litter boxes. I can't wait to see the CG cats go crazy when I burst into flames and launch myself at the wall.

Fury continues. "This is what we're starting with. We're getting all the fire burns out of the way except for Leon's. The Creature's. Which we're doing on Wednesday. After that it's just flame bars and CGI. Maybe a partial burn. I haven't decided."

Before I can stop myself, I say, "Wait, so I'm doing my Flaming Wall Scorpion today?"

Fury squints at me, as if through binoculars. "Yeah."

There's a chilling pause, until finally Target says, "Hey, good thing we're in a hospital!"

I turn and face Target, then slowly walk toward him. Something in my posture alarms the rest of the stunt team, causing them to engage, but I'm locked on Target, drilling towards him. Fury steps into my path like a blockade, and it's not until he puts his hand on my chest that I break eye contact with Target. The stunt team is gaping at me, worried, and slightly disappointed. Everyone is stunned, except Jin, who's watching me with huge, amused, *oh you're fired* eyes.

"What," I say to Jin. "His tag was sticking out."

No one reacts. The fans outside are very loud.

Fury's grin is huge and very close to my face. "Lex," he says. He slides his hand up from my chest to my shoulder and clasps it. Then he takes me into a slow hug, which somehow pulls everyone into a hug, and now they're all hugging me, one at a time, but also altogether, an awkward, slow motion mosh pit in the narrow hallway, walled in by intake folders and posters of kittens—the exact spot I'm to perform my Flaming Wall Scorpion later today.

This also happens to be the same vet clinic I bought that blow off of Raj at, ten weeks ago. The empty black parking lot is now a bright circus of film tents, two-bangers, roaring generators, and water trucks. And an ambulance, of course.

After rehearsal, I find Fury talking to Jin in the parking lot. Jin nods casually while Fury bleats like an un-milked cow, checking his Apple Watch obsessively. When they're done rallying, I approach Fury and apologize for causing a scene earlier.

"It's all good, bro!" he says.

"I don't really believe you."

"Look, Lex. I've been a little hard on you this run. I know it. But you're actually doing a pretty good job."

"Really?"

"Yeah dude. I mean, you're never working for me again. But you're doing your best, and I respect that."

"Yeah, you're never working for *me* again," I say.

Fury smiles. I realize I've never heard him laugh at a joke, other than one he told himself, and even then, not really. "Sounds good," he says. "Anything else?"

"Actually—yeah." I look around, checking behind me. "My girl Aurora is coming in next week. Any chance you can get her a role in the Cottage Fight?"

He folds his arms. "That's background casting."

"Come on, Ed. For a tight shot. Or a 'kill the monster!' or something."

"I'm not the director of that scene," he grouses.

"Alright," I say. "It's cool. Thanks."

"Is she SAG?"

"Um, yeah."

"Well, I don't know," he says. "I can't think about that now."

"Yeah, totally, I understand. Hey, Ed, you need anything? Cold brew? Trail Mix?"

"No, I'm good." He checks his Apple Watch.

"OK. Thanks, Ed."

As I turn to leave, I add, "You're gonna crush it today."

"You bet, buddy—hey, Lex!"

I turn back around.

"You've done a full body burn before, right?"

"Yes. Of course."

Fury checks his Apple Watch again. "OK good," he says. "Knock 'em dead, buddy."

At this point I don't even care about the gag. Fire burns always suck, but I really don't give a shit right now. I'll go easy on the Wall Scorpion, only get my body horizontal while the additional CG fire takes care of the visceral punch. Making it collapsible and twisted is my part. Heavy sound effects and splashing CGI is all the rest.

I tell myself this, but it's not really true. In reality, the harder you hit the ground, the better you look. Especially in Barbaric Fury. It's all in my head.

That being said, my action is pretty simple. First, we get the shot of the Fire Monster crashing through the door, and us reacting. That's all CGI.

After that, we set up for the burns. Four of us in a hallway full of fumes. We'll do the first burn two or three times for camera, then take a break and change out our fire-retardant costumes for fresh ones.

Then we'll set up for the dolly shot, where the Fire Monster charges down the hallway, casting our bodies aside like flaming corn stalks.

Fire extinguishers and aggressive yelling. Sadie, Luisa, Jin, and three others have CO_2. Two firemen hold blankets.

In the next shot—the end of the day, most likely—I'll get flung across the kitten showcase room into a Wall Scorpion. This time I can take a running lead up before launching myself headfirst into the mural—the purple kitten with a rainbow in its mouth. The wall is soft, semi-breakaway, and it should cushion my impact on the first take. After that I'll Scorpion into the concrete behind it, and they'll put a digital image of the wall there, fuck my life.

I tell myself what I always tell myself: *It's probably gonna be fine.*

Three setups with burns. Probably three takes each. Four, if one of us doesn't ignite properly. We'll have to move quickly in the hallway, because if too many accelerant fumes get into the air, it'll blow us all up. We'll have about ten seconds to get into place and ignite before it becomes dangerous.

I take a slug of CBD, wondering if the real cats miss this place, wherever they are.

Despite the heat inside the vet clinic, I've placed hand warmers in all my pockets. The undergarments I'm about to put on have been submerged in buckets of flame-retardant Zel-Jel and refrigerated to a near freezing temperature.

Over the weekend, the wardrobe department has treated our outer garments with flame retardant gel, first soaking it, then drying it—a process similar to Scotch Guarding, but for extreme temperatures. When we arrive on set, the costumes should be one hundred percent cotton, dried, and flame resistant. But we don't put them on right away. Instead, we wheel out the tubs of cold Zel-Jel and lift out our soggy thermals.

Target, Cripple, Pit Mix, and I suit up and within twenty seconds we're shivering, patting away the air bubbles under our clothes, making sure there are no dry spots. Then we put plastic raincoats on over the goop, and another layer of thermals. Finally, we put our treated costumes on over everything, and another layer of cold Zel-Jel gooped over our heads, faces, hands, boots, and props. Now the hallway smells like animal piss and eucalyptus gel and Lidocaine, and my throat is locked in revulsion.

Finally drenched with slime and fully dressed, we each take two extra fists full of Zel-Jel, in preparation for any hot spots that might flare up, presumably in the expected heat shelves, under the chin and nose, and inside the ears. Anywhere we might feel extreme heat, we swat with a glob of all-natural cooling gel.

When the cameras are rolling and sound speeds, we scramble into position. Special FX has wheeled the fire cannon to the end of the hallway, where the Fire Monster will later be inserted digitally. The fire cannon is a propane tank with a pipe attached to it that will blast an orange wad of flames down the length of the hallway. The walls and ceiling have been wetted down by the special FX department with a flame-resistant water-nitrogen mixture.

Now we're standing on our marks, and the fire team rushes in to paint us down with flame accelerant, slathering the gluey substance all over us as hastily as possible. Sadie and Luisa are behind them, holding spray bottles full of gasoline.

As Sadie spritzes my thighs with gasoline, she winks up at me and whispers, "Hail Satan."

I don't smile, but I manage an amazingly convincing, "Fuck yeah," which might've been too loud because my ears are packed with jelly.

The fire team scatters, and Ed Fury, standing next to the fire cannon screams, "Stunts, set! Everybody take a deep breath!

"In . . . THREE, TWO, ONE, *ACTION!*"

The fire cannon explodes with a muffled "whump," and the four of us burst into flames. We flail around like monkeys for nine seconds, then lie down on the floor in a Christ-on-a-cross position.

"GET 'EM GET 'EM GET 'EM GET 'EM!" Fury screams, and six fire extinguishers go full blast. Within seconds the hallway is a solid mass of carbon dioxide. The firemen are holding blankets, but they can't see anything, and someone steps on my hand with an audible *crunch*.

After cleaning and rewetting the hallway, we do this action two more times. Eventually our fire repellant wears down, and we're forced to strip off our thermals and suit up again for the next shot.

It's the same setup as before: fire cannon, singular propane fireball, accelerant glue, and a light spritz of gasoline on our thighs. Only this time the camera is on a push dolly, simulating the point of view of the Fire Monster as it charges down the hallway. Everyone does their wreck except for me. My wreck is in the next shot, after lunch.

After lunch, I'm back in my thermals, slimy and shivering in the hallway near the kitten showroom. The reek of eucalyptus freezes my brain.

Ed Fury is upset. Through my impatience I can see him aggressing Jin Hoon and the cinematographer, waving his hands in what looks like near panic. Patricia stands a few feet away, typing on her iPad, but I can tell she's listening in on them.

Leon shoulders up to me and says, "You OK, bro?"

"Yup, tippy top," I say, watching Ed Fury.

"Did you hear the news?"

"No. I don't like the news."

"Comedy Central, bro. *Limited* theatrical release. Not even Netflix. The whole thing is fucked."

I don't say anything. It's far too late for me to care.

"Ben Schilling's busting heads right now. Talking to his manager and shit."

"You're fucking with me, Leon. It's not working. I don't care."

"It's true, bro!"

"Impossible," I say. "The budget's too high."

"That's the point! They're cutting like forty million in advertising and distribution. Schilling's busting heads right now!" Leon looks around, making sure he isn't overheard. The crew members in the hallway appear disgruntled, on edge. I just stare at him through a mask of grey slime.

"But that's not all, bro." Leon leans in close, so he's almost whispering. "Bro," he says. "Fury's wife just kicked him out."

My heart drops finally, as I realize I never hated Ed Fury. To avoid comment I say, "Really?"

"Yeah, bro. The times, they are a-changin'."

I want to slump against the wall. There isn't a single Bob Dylan lyric in thirty-four albums that can disentangle what's happening.

"Man, Leon, you don't get it," I say at last.

"What do you mean?"

"You don't understand this," I gesture with an arm made of ectoplasm. "You don't understand *me*. You're not afraid of pain. You're not an addict. You're not nearing middle-age, and you don't have herniations in your spine. You have no inner conflict. You're just a . . . I don't even know what you are. I don't understand you, either."

After a moment Leon stops shifting and says, "My dad abandoned me, bro." He looks down at his feet, then back at me. "And my stepdad abused my mom and me. Because of that, I always believed I was unwanted. That's why I'm a stuntman. It's a show of competence. I'm part of a team. And I won't be disarmed, ever."

I'm about to say something stupid when Leon looks past me, realizes something, and quickly walks away. Jin Hoon appears in his place and starts patting down my body, getting the oxygen bubbles out of the gel-soaked thermals. Nobody wants air bubbles in their underwear during a fire burn. They're like little bombs. I wonder if there's enough alcohol in my blood to completely explode.

Target approaches us, half smiling as always. He changed into his street clothes during lunch. He stands directly in front of me and says something supportive like, "Lex, you're a fucking legend," but I don't hear him. I'm staring at the purple kitten with the rainbow in its mouth painted on the wall, unnerved by the way it's looking at me. Its eyes are flat, and its grin seems to know too much. The kitten is goading me. "You're the Wall Scorpion," it says. "And I'm the motherfucking wall."

You're a breakaway wall, I argue, thousand-yard staring at the purple kitten. We get lost outside of ourselves when we're this physically uncomfortable. I'm coated with cold sludge, wearing elbow pads and baseball sliders, breathing fumes. I want to get out of this. I've wired myself completely wrong. This is my own fault. No, my own *design.* Stuntmen exist in a kind of self-sustained biome, and once an aesthetic is cast, it becomes ubiquitous, and everyone is caught in the web.

"I'm not supposed to be here," I say. But nobody hears me.

The grinning kitten knows that my masterpiece is set to explode, and it's all due to my own faulty wiring. Jin's not lighting me on fire. I am. I've already ingested the pill, and now it's kicking in. And here in the moment, ultimately called to arms, I just want it to stop.

My mind flashes on Wolfblood, eating a poisoned rat.

But then I think about Aurora, and I'm an optimist again. She's coming tomorrow, and even though she's not here now, the thought gives me comfort.

Target notices my trance and says, "Fucking weirdo." He punches my shoulder lightly as he walks away, wiping his knuckles on his jeans.

Ben Schilling approaches me (what is this, a going away party?) and makes a lewd joke about my slimy condition. I think he tells me he loves me, but I'm still zoning out on the purple kitten, because now my initial shoot-me nonchalance as well as my subsequent hope for Aurora are both gone, and in their place are the tentacles. Cold, clutching tendrils of anxiety have vined their way around my torso, beneath all the fireproof layers, and my temples are suddenly freezing. The spotlight I'm projecting on the grinning kitten dims. I have no idea why I should be nervous, let alone holding in a scream. My action is easy. The camera is right there! It's not going to move. All I have to do is start out of frame, then run in and wreck. It's the easiest setup in the world, for a stuntman.

Dread causes my hands to shake, as I realize I'm in over my head. Although I feel defeated, I have no idea who the victor is. It isn't faulty wiring, it isn't the stunt industry, and it isn't Ed Fury.

It's age, I guess. It's time. Time is a river that washes all the cartilage out of our bones. It carries the strength from our hearts. Now, I'm nothing more than a skeleton, held together by misbelief. The only way out is through that break-away wall.

Come at me, chicken.

Before we roll, the fire cannon is wheeled noisily past us and outside. I look down at the floor and gasp, taking an involuntary step backwards, sneering as if at some horrible ledge I hadn't known I was standing on.

"You good?" Jin says.

I don't respond. A single blue streak has marked the floor in front of me. The streak alarms me of something, but I can't remember what. Pointing a finger at the floor, with my mouth completely dry, I can only look at Jin and hopelessly mutter, "Um . . ."

Jin looks down. "What," he says. "That's from the fire cannon. The wheel's fucked up."

I continue to gawk at Jin through a mask of slime, my mouth opening and closing wordlessly like a fish.

"I like you, Lex. But you're a fucking weirdo."

"Still rolling, guys," someone says.

"You good?" Jin asks again. "We gotta go. The fumes are gonna—"

"I'm fucking set, let's do it," I say.

"One take, buddy, you got this."

"Let's fucking go."

"I'll call action when you're fully lit. After that it's your own timing."

"Fuck you, let's go!"

"You set?"

"SET!"

"OK!" he says. "TAKE A DEEP BREATH!"

I take a deep breath and hold it.

Jin picks a blowtorch up off the floor and screams, "HERE WE GO!"

He ignites me in three places. Within seconds I'm fully engulfed.

"AND—*ACTION!*"

I charge into the showroom and leap headfirst into the wall. The breakaway wall does not cave in. Instead, there's a loud snap in my neck which causes my feet to kick spasmodically in the air, and my teeth go down my throat. Before I can choke, or even cough, I lose all sensation. The world doesn't blackout all at once, but rather slowly, like house lights dimming in a large theater, as the curtain rises over some cavernous stage, a glittering world where nothing is real, and everything is ethereal, and before I know it, I'm

BLOODY REMAINS

HI, THIS IS Ben Schilling, the actor. Nice to meet you. Prayers and greetings.

You're probably wondering how the last few pages of this story were written, given the fact that Lex Mercier fell tragically in the final chapter. I suppose I should tell you: the last few pages were written by me. I'd like to let you know how that happened, so you don't think this whole thing's a sham, which it's not.

Bananas, yes. But a sham, no.

On the morning after Lex's death, Aurora arrived at the Wollcroft Hotel. Miss Jenny had been expecting her, and she gave Aurora a key to room 626 without any hassle. Neither Aurora nor Miss Jenny had been informed of the recent tragedy. It had only occurred five hours prior to Aurora's arrival and was still under wraps. A police investigation had begun, and soon the world would be frenzying about it, blowing up the internet, but for now, there was only silence.

Aurora was later seen stumbling through the courtyard of the Wollcroft Hotel around 9:30 a.m. Members of the stunt team were drinking beer at a table, quietly processing the horror they had just witnessed, when Aurora recognized them as film people (biceps, ball caps, and the word STUNTS on all their clothes). She approached them and asked if they were working on *Everyone's Frankenstein*. When they nodded their solemn heads, Aurora pointed one trembling arm in the direction of Lex's room, high up in the corner, and collapsed.

A few minutes later, Aurora came to. Refusing to be taken to a hospital, she, along with Leon and Miss Jenny, went back to Lex's room. Aurora appeared to be in shock. Her skin was white wax, and she was unable to speak.

Wolfblood was in a paper bag, tucked into a drawer underneath the television. She appeared to have been dead a long time. The smell inside the room was cloying, even with the window tragically slanted open.

We would find out later from police reports that Wolfblood, AKA "Bloody," had been dead somewhere between five and six weeks. Cause of death: anticoagulant rodenticide, via relay toxicosis. Ingestion of poisoned rat.

Lex's room was in disarray. The fridge was full of mold, blood was on the floor, and loose papers and hundreds of index cards were scattered everywhere.

No drugs, nor any trace of drugs or alcohol were found in Lex's hotel room. The toxicology report included in his autopsy yielded the same empty-handed result. The autopsy had been requested for liability purposes, paid for by Universal's high-risk production insurance, and the results were shared with the police investigation.

A few days after Lex's passing, my stunt double Leon Williams handed me a stack of papers that he found in Lex's hotel room. The stack was crumpled and weirdly stained. People always give me stuff because I'm a famous actor.

A month went by which I spent sitting and sulking, not reading any new scripts. I liked Lex. He had a good sense of humor and a creative, professional edge that was fun to be around (most of the time). Eventually, I put this book together. Lex had a working title, which I found to be terrible. He called it *Hostel Mind,* which would've been impossible to Google, because "hostel" would have to be deliberately misspelled. I reworked the title, decided to go with *The Stunted Man.* Because come on, it works three ways.

I finished the last chapter to tie the ends together. I wrote it from the point of view of a man who was not suicidal. Despite his struggles with addiction and depression, I don't believe Lex had any intention of hurting himself. He was a fighter, disguised as a drinker, and underneath it all he was as hard as stone. Or in his case, as hard as Cannibal Corpse's fourth album.

I showed the book to David Morley, and he told me I should publish it. I set out to do so without hesitation. And the film, *Everyone's Frankenstein* is dedicated to Lex, by Morley, on behalf of the crew and everyone who knew him.

Morley continues to work with Ed Fury. Fury is not such a bad guy, by the way. He's been hugely satirized in Lex's telling. Lex was a dramatic man, and a good storyteller in that way.

I don't take any credit for this book, although I am proud to have had it printed. I think it paints Hollywood with a textured, ancient kind of brush stroke. We are people, anyway. Soft on the inside, spiky on the surface. We work for the man, and we suffer for the craft. We put up with one another for grueling lengths of time. Getting along, speaking the same language, and sometimes patronizing people is half the battle. Patience ebbs more than flows. Maybe that's what the Covid masks were suggesting. They didn't need to be in the story, but Lex put them in there, explaining that he never knew who was talking on set, or what their emotional temperature was, or what facial readings he couldn't get from anyone. Language is not our first language, after all. Lex's connection to the world had become untethered, and perhaps that is what sent him into such a chaotic delirium.

Moviemaking is not exactly as it's portrayed in the books and the films. All that glamour—starlets and clapperboards, men hauling enormous lights through sun-drenched studio lots, palm trees and convertibles, sharp-witted producers in meetings, comedic conversations at crafty, and mild PG-rated debauchery. It's all bullshit. Filmmakers are beautiful, often desperate human beings, working hard to get it done against terrible odds. Crew members die sometimes.

People have miscarriages, divorces, and seizures on set, sometimes while cameras are rolling. On many of the films I've worked on, a crew member was diagnosed with cancer.

I encourage you to go out and watch *Everyone's Frankenstein*. It's a good film. I was wary about David at the start, but I thought it turned out great. Bring a pint of beer with you, or a pint of whiskey. And when you see the Dead Assassin do his cape flip, pop that sucker open and take a drink. And remember that life is short. Sometimes, stunted. Enjoy it as much as you can. Follow your heart, even if it leads you directly into the family boneyard. You're headed that way anyways, so you might as well enjoy the ride. If you live fast, you'll find plenty of time to take breaks and enjoy the scenery.

I believe that if Lex had one more thing to say, it would be this: Don't be afraid of earthquakes. There are other ways to get crushed and die in this world.

✝

THE END
7/2022 — 7/2023

PRAISE FOR *THUNDER, AZ:*

WINNER:

Jack Eadon Memorial Award for Best Contemporary Drama

FIRST PLACE:

Firebird Book Award (Horror)
Reader Views (Horror / Western)

"Engrossing . . . Complete annihilation . . . An unforgettable tale that has never been told before."
—*Paige Lovitt*

"Pendulum rides, freak shows, and the best damn shooting gallery. You'll grin, gasp, and line up for more."
—*Glen Berger*

"Loeb creates a true feeling of dread and death. All horror lovers will agree."
—*Reader Views*

Order your copy today:
https://a.co/d/hkXrpga
www.ariloeb.com

ARI LOEB

Ari Loeb grew up as a dancer and acrobat, touring with companies such as Cirque du Soleil, Momix, and Pilobolus. He later worked as a choreographer and performer on the Broadway musical, *Spider-Man: Turn Off the Dark*. Ari choreographed for television programs in Spain, Italy, Canada, Dubai, Sweden, and the United States. After many years in New York City and on the road, he returned to his hometown, Los Angeles, pursuing a career in stunts, and he has since worked on over one hundred films, television shows and video games, specializing in creature horror, such as *Fear The Walking Dead, Zombieland: Double-Tap, Renfield,* and the *Resident Evil* franchise. His debut novel, *Thunder, Az* is an award-winning piece of survival horror.